STRIKER

K19 SECURITY SOLUTIONS

BOOK SIX

HEATHER SLADE

STRIKER

This book is a work of fiction. The names, characters, places and incidents are products of the writer's imagination or have been used fictitiously and are not to be construed as real. Any resemblance to persons, living or dead, actual events, locale or organizations is entirely coincidental.

Paperback:
ISBN-13: 978-1-942200-59-8
ISBN-10: 1-942200-59-5

MORE FROM AUTHOR HEATHER SLADE

BUTLER RANCH
Prequel: *Kade's Worth*
Book One: *Brodie*
Book Two: *Maddox*
Book Three: *Naughton*
Book Four: *Mercer*
Book Five: *Kade*

K19 SECURITY SOLUTIONS
Book One: *Razor*
Book Two: *Gunner*
Book Three: *Mistletoe*
Book Four: *Mantis*
Book Five: *Dutch*
Book Six: *Striker*
Book Seven: *Monk*
Book Eight: *Halo*
Book Nine: *Tackle*
Coming soon:
Book Ten: *Onyx*

MILITARY INTELLIGENCE SECTION 6
Book One: *Shiver*
Book Two: *Wilder*
Book Three: *Pinch*
Book Four: *Shadow*

THE INVINCIBLES
Book One: *Decked*
Book Two: *Edged*
Book Three: *Grinded*
Book Four: *Riled*
Book Five: *Smoked*
Book Six: *Bucked*
Coming soon:
Book Seven: *Irished*

ROARING FORK RANCH
Coming soon:
Book One: *Roughstock*
Book Two: *Rockstar*

COWBOYS OF CRESTED BUTTE
Book One: *Fall for Me*
Book Two: *Dance with Me*
Book Three: *Kiss Me Cowboy*
Book Four: *Stay with Me*
Book Five: *Win Me Over*

COCKY HERO CLUB
Undercover Agent

KB WORLDS
EVERYDAY HEROES:
Handled

Table of Contents

1

Striker

I was ready to throw my phone against the wall of the office in my McLean, Virginia, condo.

"Why are you surprised? I told you this would happen when you allowed Ghafor to go to Colombia," I shouted at Kellen "Money" McTiernan, the man who had taken my job at the CIA when I left.

"The United States' relationship with Colombia is stable now and was then, Griffin. There was no reason to refuse to let Ghafor go wherever he wanted to, as long as it wasn't back to Pakistan," McTiernan shot back.

There were at least three things in Money's statement that pissed me off. Telling me anything about US–Colombian relations was his first mistake. I'd been the CIA's resident expert on not just Colombia, but all of South America before I left the agency.

Calling me Griffin, rather than Striker, was his second error. There were very few people who got away with calling me that, and Money wasn't one of them.

Finally, saying there wasn't any reason Ghafor, former leader of the Islamic State, should've been permitted to go anywhere that wasn't a prison cell or a morgue, made my blood pressure skyrocket.

"Where do you think he is now?"

"We're not certain he's in Pakistan."

"You're not *certain*. Is that what you just said? I thought you were supposed to have a genius-level IQ. Evidently, that is a misconception. *Of course he's in Pakistan, you idiot.*"

Abdul Ghafor was the shit beneath the shoe of the worst scumbag on the face of the earth. He was personally responsible for the deaths of several American operatives, along with playing an integral role in the fraudulent presidential election that had resulted in a man who never should've been elected to one term in office, let alone two, taking oath.

That man would soon be impeached, and if the universe didn't screw it up somehow, once he was out of office, he'd also be prosecuted and sent to prison.

It didn't matter to me that Ghafor's testimony had led to several other indictments of election fraud and money laundering; that the State Department let the man live was an affront to everything I believed in. Shipping him off to Buenaventura, Colombia, a hotbed of Islamic fundamentalism, was akin to asking for another catastrophic attack on US soil.

I put my hand over the mic on my phone when Owen "Ranger" Messick walked into my office followed by Caleb "Diesel" Jacks.

"Money *thinks* Ghafor *might* have returned to Pakistan."

The look on both Ranger's and Diesel's faces clearly conveyed that they shared the same opinion of McTiernan I did.

"You'll receive the briefing tomorrow at zero eight hundred," Money said right before he disconnected the call.

"That *sonuvabitch* hung up on me," I said, once again tempted to throw my phone. With my luck, I'd put a hole in the wall, and it would be one more thing I'd have to repair before I sold the condo I rarely lived in. At least not since Aine McNamara and I had broken up.

"You ready to head out, boss?" asked Diesel, propping his feet on my desk.

Before I could do it myself, Ranger reached over and knocked Diesel's feet off.

"I'm not your boss," I grumbled, although at times like these, I wished I'd never left the agency. No way in hell would Ghafor have disappeared on my watch.

"What's Doc told you about the meeting?" asked Ranger.

"Only that it's tomorrow in Yachats."

Just saying the name of the small coastal town in Oregon made my chest hurt.

Why the hell did Doc Butler need us to meet there of all places? K19 Security Solutions' senior partner had a wide range of options when he called a meeting of the other senior and junior partners—like I was. In the past, we'd always met on the Central Coast of California, where all four founding partners owned houses even if they didn't live there full-time.

Doc's choice of Yachats for this meeting was baffling, particularly since Razor Sharp was the only member of the team who had a permanent residence there.

Regardless, my main hope was that during the short time I planned to be in town, I could manage to avoid running into Aine McNamara.

Whatever information I'd anticipated getting in advance of the K19 team meeting was thwarted by whom Razor had sent to pick up Ranger, Diesel, and me from the airport.

Rhys "Monk" Perrin was the least talkative man I'd ever met. Usually, it didn't bother me. It seemed like most people talked more to hear the sound of their own voice than to say anything of importance. When I needed information though, it was irritating as hell.

What I really wanted to know wasn't about the meeting. I wanted to know how Aine was, although even if Monk were a chatterbox, I never would've asked him about her.

I had my own man on reconnaissance, someone I'd worked with at the agency who did private investigation work on the side. I'd hired Halo to make sure Aine didn't get herself into any danger. When I received word that she was dating a local guy, I'd thought about backing off, but hadn't been able to bring myself to. I told Halo to limit his reports to essential information only, not because I wasn't concerned anymore; it just hurt too much to think about her with another man.

"Why did you turn here?" I asked, realizing Monk had made a left onto the street that would take us to Razor's place rather than to the hotel.

"Going to the house."

"I figured that. What I want to know is why?"

"This is where Razor told me to bring you."

I didn't bother looking at either Ranger or Diesel sitting in the back seat; I could hear them snickering.

2

Aine

"What did you say?" I asked my twin, Ava.

"The K19 team is meeting here tomorrow."

"Here? At the house?" While I didn't live with my sister and brother-in-law, I lived in the house next door, which was close enough.

Ava shook her head. "No, at the Overleaf. I think that's where everyone's staying."

"What do you mean by everyone?"

"I don't know whether Griffin is coming or not."

I'd tell Ava that wasn't what I meant, but I'd be lying. "It's inevitable that we'll see each other," I said instead.

"Maybe." Ava shrugged. "What did you and Stuart do this weekend?"

"Dinner and a movie."

Stuart was a great guy. He was handsome, well educated, ran his own business in town—granted, it was a plumbing business—but still, it was his.

Was he the hottest man I'd ever dated? No. Did he make every nerve ending in my body stand up and take notice? Never. However, he also hadn't broken my heart, and likely never would. Stuart made no secret that if he thought there was any chance I'd say yes, he'd propose to me tomorrow.

"Aine?"

"What?"

"I asked you a question," Ava said with a hand on her hip.

"Sorry. I didn't hear you."

"What movie, and where did you go to dinner?"

"Um, some spy movie, and we ate at the brewery. Listen, I'm supposed to meet Mom for a pedicure. I'll catch up with you later."

I wasn't supposed to meet our mother until this afternoon, but it was the only thing I could think of to get away from Ava and give myself time to think.

A year ago, Griffin Ellis—whom I should start calling Striker like everyone else—and I were embarking on what I thought was going to be a serious relationship. We'd spent Thanksgiving together, and even though he'd been on a mission, he made it home on Christmas Day to be with me. Between then and the end of February, I'd all but moved into his McLean, Virginia, condominium.

At the beginning of March, things fell apart. I still had a hard time processing what had happened, not that it mattered now. It was over, and while my heart hadn't accepted it yet, my brain was at least partially on board.

I only hoped that I could manage to avoid running into Striker Ellis while he was in town.

3

Striker

"I thought we weren't meeting until tomorrow," I said to Razor when the man opened the front door.

Razor ignored me but shook hands with Ranger and Diesel. "Did you review the proposal Merrigan sent over?" he asked them.

While I didn't know what the proposal said exactly, my assumption was that Doc's wife, K19's managing director, was offering each of the former CIA agents a job. Maybe that's why Monk brought us here instead of the hotel. If that was the case, I wondered if I could beg off and go to the Overleaf on my own.

I was about to ask when Razor turned his head. I followed the man's gaze over to where his wife, Aine's identical twin sister, sat, holding a baby. Her likeness caused a heaviness to settle on my chest.

"How's he doing, Avarie?" Razor asked.

"He's fine. I guess I shouldn't have eaten that leftover Indian food for lunch. Could you hold him for a minute?" she asked.

"Come meet the guys," Razor said, taking the baby from her arms and walking over to where I stood with Ranger and Diesel.

"This is Tabon Samual Sharp VI, who we call Sam."

Neither of the other two guys seemed to know what to do any more than I did.

"You wanna hold him?" Razor asked.

No, I didn't want to hold a damn baby. *WTF?*

Razor laughed out loud. "You should see your face right now."

"I got a nephew who's six months," said Diesel, sounding as awkward as I felt and Ranger looked.

"Sam is four months."

I shifted on my feet, wondering how long we'd have to talk about a little human who was presently drooling so much that the neck of his tiny shirt was wet.

Ava came back and took the baby from Razor's arms. "How are you, Striker?"

"Good, thanks. Do you know Ranger and Diesel?"

Ava nodded and said hello before turning back to me. "Can I talk to you for a minute?"

"Sure," I said, following her into the kitchen. "Look—"

Ava held up her hand. "Before you say anything, I just want you to know that Aine is seeing someone."

The heaviness I'd felt before, thinking about how much Ava and her sister looked alike, was now a boulder on my chest, realizing how much they sounded alike too.

"I hope she's happy," I responded after enough time had passed that Ava was staring at me.

"I hope so too."

"I won't be in town long," I added, although I wasn't sure why. Maybe so she could reassure her sister.

"We'll make that decision once Doc and Merrigan get here," said Razor, joining us.

"What's with all the mystery?" asked Ranger, saying out loud what I was thinking.

Razor motioned us out of the kitchen then went back in and kissed Ava's cheek and the baby's head.

I turned away, but not before I saw the sweet smile Razor's wife gave him. Aine had the same smile, and the warmth I felt when she looked at me that way was probably how Razor was feeling right then. God, I missed it.

"I've got a new setup downstairs I want to familiarize you with. It's also in the house in Cambria, almost identical to this."

The last time I was downstairs, there had been a large workout room, a small office, and a huge storage area. Now the "office," if it could be called that, was three times the size of the workout room, and the storage area appeared to be nonexistent.

"Wow," I muttered, marveling at all the equipment packed into the space. There were times K19's technology budget blew my mind. The fact that we didn't have to jump through hoops for funding meant the equipment we had would be what the agency might acquire months from now.

"Come on, show it off," Razor said to Monk, who was already sitting in front of one of the monitors.

"What software is this?" asked Diesel, leaning in.

"Same technology used for the drones," answered Razor.

"What are we looking at?"

"Ghafor's compound in Pakistan."

I shook my head. I'd had no doubt that's where the bastard was, not that the CIA was willing to admit their mistake.

"Can you zoom in there?" I asked Monk, pointing to the screen.

"I thought he was out of money," said Ranger, noticing the same thing I had. The man was stockpiling munitions.

"He's been receiving regular shipments of arms at this location. Which means somebody's funding him."

My disgust at the CIA's decision intensified. Allowing Ghafor to pick his place of exile had to be one of the stupidest moves I'd ever seen them make. It wouldn't take a genius to figure out that the Islamic fundamentalists also living in exile in Colombia gave Abdul the money he needed to get back on his feet. The Islamic State appeared to be gearing up for something significant, and until I could figure out what, we needed to wait and watch the bastard.

Razor looked at his watch. "Doc and Merrigan should be here within an hour."

"Then what?"

"Dinner."

4

Aine

I was in my sister's kitchen with our mother, who was holding Sam, when I heard voices from the other room. One voice in particular sent a chill up my spine.

"I thought you said they were staying at the Overleaf."

"They are, but we're having dinner at the house tonight."

"I see."

Ava sighed. "Aine, you dated him for what, four months?"

"What's your point?"

"My point is, you're seeing someone else now, and you aren't a four-year-old. Get over it."

I didn't respond. Instead, I leaned down, kissed Sam and then my mother's cheek, and hugged her. "Have a great time on the cruise. What time is Stan picking you up?"

"A little before seven in the morning. I'll try not to wake you."

I nodded, hugged my mother again, and then walked out the back door of the house without saying another word to Ava. I was about to go in my own front door when I saw Stuart pull into the driveway.

"Hey, pretty girl," he said, climbing out of his truck.

"Stuart, I wasn't expecting you."

"I finished the job I was on earlier than I thought I would."

"Do you want to come in?"

"Have you had dinner?"

I shook my head.

"Good. I made a reservation."

"Where?"

"It's a surprise."

I smiled. This was exactly what I needed—a night out with my current boyfriend would help me forget about the one who came before him.

"Let me change." I pointed to a spot on my shirt where Sam had spit up.

"I'll be out on the trail."

I watched Stuart walk out to the bench that sat between the house I shared with my mother and the Pacific Ocean. November was one of the best times of the year to see gray whales as they began their migration south. Between now and mid-January, over eighteen thousand would travel between their northern feeding grounds to Baja California, where the warm-water lagoons would become nurseries for expectant females.

Even though it was chilly, Stuart and I often walked to dinner, whale-watching along the way.

I put on a pair of flannel-lined jeans, a wool sweater, and a down jacket. Stuart, who'd lived in Yachats all his life, wasn't as sensitive to the cold as I was, but he never gave me a hard time about it.

"Ready?" he asked when I joined him on the trail. I turned to go south, to town, but Stuart grabbed my hand. "Our reservation is this way." He smiled and pulled me in the opposite direction.

There was only one restaurant north of where we lived that was within walking distance—the Overleaf.

I'd suggest we go somewhere else, but getting a reservation at the restaurant with the best view of the coastline was hard to come by. In fact, how had he when he thought he was going to have to work late?

"What's the occasion?"

"I saved the owner's ass, and in exchange, he gave me his table for dinner tonight."

I looked down at my jeans. "I'm not really dressed for a fancy dinner."

"This is Yachats, Aine. You know no one dresses for dinner."

I tried hard not to look at Ava and Razor's house as we passed by, but failed.

Sure enough, my fear of humiliation manifested itself when I saw Striker standing out on the deck and our eyes met. I waved, looked away, and picked up my pace.

"Who was that?" asked Stuart.

"Just someone who works with my brother-in-law."

5

Striker

Seeing Aine with another man didn't hurt as bad as I thought it would—it hurt a hell of a lot worse.

She looked happy, though, didn't she? The split second when our eyes met hadn't given me enough time to say for sure.

I watched her walk away with Stuart Anderson, owner of Anderson's Plumbing and all around "nice" guy. Stuart's age had bothered me when I looked him up, but at thirty-one, he was seven years my junior, and instead of being sixteen years older than Aine, Stuart was only nine.

Monk came out the slider and handed me a beer. "Thought you might need one," he said.

"Thanks, man. I must look pretty miserable for you to string five whole words together."

Monk flipped me off and took a swig of his own beer. "The reason I don't laugh at everyone's jokes about how I never talk isn't because I'm shy or whatever the hell you all think about me; it's because they stopped being funny years ago."

"I know. It's just easier to give you shit than it is to face how effed up my own life is."

Monk nodded. "Saylor and I went out for dinner with them a couple of weeks ago."

Saylor was Razor's sister, and I'd heard that she and Monk were spending time together, but I didn't know to what extent. "Aine and Stu?"

"Yeah, but don't call him Stu. He hates it."

"Were you the offending party?"

"Nah, someone else at the brewery said it."

I scrubbed my face with my hand. "I can't believe I'm saying this, Monk, but does she seem happy?"

"He's a plumber."

I turned my head and studied him. "So?"

"You're a former CIA agent who is now a partner in a private intelligence firm. You oughta be able to figure it out." Monk held up his empty bottle. "Want another?"

I nodded. "Thanks, man."

The sun was just about to set on a day I'd been avoiding for eight months. I knew I'd see Aine McNamara again since her sister was married to one of K19's founding partners. I'd just hoped I could finagle my way out of it for several more weeks, or even months. Long enough that I could be certain she'd moved on and was happy. If she hadn't, or wasn't, I might be tempted to tell her that

I'd made a horrible mistake when I ended things, and beg her to take me back.

I couldn't do that, though; I was every kind of bad for Aine. She deserved to be with someone who was closer to her own age, someone whom she could build a life with rather than jump into one that was already established. Also, someone who didn't travel ninety percent of the time. The plumber probably never traveled, at least not for work.

There were other reasons we couldn't be together, but I hadn't told her that.

Monk came out to the deck, handed me the beer, and then went back inside, leaving me alone with my thoughts. It was a place where I really didn't want to be, so I went inside too.

"Doc and Merrigan have been delayed. They'll arrive at zero seven hundred tomorrow," said Razor. "You can hang out here and eat or go to the hotel, whichever you'd prefer."

Ranger and Diesel motioned with their heads to leave, and I was happy to join them. It had been a long day, and we were on East Coast time, so it was three hours later for us.

"You can take the SUV," said Monk, handing me the key.

"Can we give you a lift somewhere?" I asked him.

"No, thanks."

Monk was back to his uncommunicative self, but I didn't care. All I wanted to do was go to the hotel and sleep. I just hoped I could, and if I did, I wouldn't dream about Aine.

When I walked into the entrance of the hotel, the first thing I saw was Aine seated at a table with the plumber. A few moments later, two other men joined them at the same time "Stu" gripped the back of her neck with his hand.

I kept watching them, even when Ranger and Diesel walked over to the front desk to check in.

Her profile was illuminated by the table's candlelight, making her look like an angel. As if I'd called out to her, Aine shrugged the plumber's hand away, slowly turned her head, and looked at me. There was no way she could assume I was doing anything other than staring at her.

Our eyes stayed focused on one another's until I saw the plumber about to turn his head. I tore my gaze away and joined Ranger and Diesel at the front desk.

Something about her haunted look before she'd turned toward me ate away at me. What weighed so heavily on her mind? It couldn't be me; she'd obviously moved on with Stu.

Other things that had happened in her life haunted her. Did the plumber know all the trauma she'd been through in the last couple of years? Did he know that her father had lied about his identity her entire life? Did he know that she'd been kidnapped along with two of her closest friends and was held hostage in order to lure out the same man? Did he know she had nightmares nearly every night?

He probably did, and that part was too much for me to think about. The idea that my sweet Aine would lay naked in someone else's arms made every muscle in my body clutch in anger. If only I could own her mewls of pleasure. I closed my eyes, remembering.

* * *

After almost losing my life in Somalia, I'd done everything I could to get back to the States for Christmas. It wasn't as early in the day as I would've liked, but it wasn't too late for Aine and me to celebrate together.

I whisked her away from where she was staying in Annapolis and drove her to my condo in McLean, Virginia.

Once there, the first thing we did was exchange gifts. I gave her a garnet bracelet that had belonged to the only relative who had ever truly cared about me: my aunt, Dorothy. Coincidentally, my aunt and Aine shared the same birthday: the third of January.

She gave me what I thought was a pocket watch, but when I opened the cover, I saw it was a compass with a message engraved on the inside.

If you take me by the hand
Open your heart
I'll help you
Find your way back home.
A.

"Is it silly for me to say this is the best Christmas I've ever had?" she asked when I told her how much I loved it.

"Not at all. It's the best Christmas I've ever had too."

I stroked her cheek with my fingertip. "Are you hungry?"

Aine's cheeks flushed, and she turned her head.

"Tell me what you're thinking."

"Not for food."

I lifted Aine in my arms and carried her up the stairs, telling her all the way how much I'd missed her.

I lowered her to the bed and knelt in front of her, pushing the sweater she wore up so she'd take it off. I leaned forward and kissed the pale skin above the red lace bra that held the two most perfect breasts I'd ever seen.

Aine gasped when I pulled the cups down, exposing her nipples. I took one into my mouth while my fingers toyed with the other, pinching and then stroking the pebbled nub.

"Lie back."

"Griffin—"

"Shh," I whispered, unfastening her jeans and sliding them over her hips. I left the red lace panties on that matched her bra, and kissed through their dampness.

"Every time I closed my eyes, this is what I thought about," I murmured as I pulled the panties to the side and feasted on her pussy.

No woman I'd ever been with responded to me the way Aine did, and no other woman had turned me on the way she did, either.

***

God, I missed her. Not only in my bed, but in every part of my life. What could I do, though? I'd made the decision to end our relationship.

6

Aine

Two of Stuart's friends stopped by the table, and after about a minute, I lost interest in their conversation.

Why couldn't I have stopped myself from looking at the house when we'd walked by? And why did Striker have to be standing out on the deck? Why did we have to make eye contact? Couldn't he have looked away?

Stuart rested his hand on my leg. When I smiled, he moved it to the back of my neck.

"Bored?" he asked, leaning in to kiss the side of my face.

I shook my head. "I'm fine."

Stuart smiled and continued talking with his friends. He kept his hand on my neck, though. It felt possessive, and not in a good way. More as though he wanted to be sure I stayed focused on him while he was in a conversation that had nothing to do with me.

I wouldn't have had to turn and look; I felt Striker's presence as soon as he walked through the hotel's entrance. The air changed. It wasn't warmer or colder; it was heavier—thick with so many things left unsaid.

There were endless questions I wanted to ask. Why had he suddenly decided he was so wrong for me after we'd talked about everything from our age difference to how often he was forced to be away because of what he did for a living?

These were two of the things he'd pointed out as reasons a relationship couldn't work between us. Something told me, though, that there was more to it.

I had a slew of insecurities I could turn into other reasons he didn't want to be with me.

But why did the air still crackle when the only connection between us was through our eyes? What would it be like if we spoke? Would the pull be too much for us to ignore, or were those feelings mine alone? Maybe he was immune to what I believed was an undeniable attraction, or maybe he didn't feel it the way I did.

I turned my head and saw Stuart's two friends had left and that he'd seen Striker and me staring at each other.

"Someone your brother-in-law works with," he said, his eyes boring into mine.

"That's right."

"I wish you'd tell me the truth, Aine."

"I'm not lying to you. That's all he is." While he may have played a different role in my life at one time, now he was just someone my sister's husband worked with.

"Not hungry?" Stuart asked, eyeing my half-eaten plate.

"Not as much as I thought." I'd ordered a smaller-portion meal, knowing the anxiety I felt over Striker being in Yachats would ruin my appetite.

Stuart motioned to the waiter for the check.

"Let me get it." I pulled my wallet out of my small cross-body bag.

"Aine, please don't do that."

"You shouldn't have to pay every time we go out."

"I'm happy to."

Stuart and I hadn't discussed finances, but I knew there were times when his business was booming and then times he didn't work for several days in a row.

I, on the other hand, had more money than I could spend in a lifetime, unless I gave it all away, which I'd considered doing more than once.

"It's dirty money," I said to my mother one day after I'd gotten off the phone with the trustee who'd managed Ava's and my money for most of our lives. The man was connected to the investment firm that held our assets, rather than to our father. If it had been the other way around, neither Ava nor I would have a penny to our name.

"Consider it a small compensation for the hell your father put you through," my mother had said that day.

No amount of money could erase that horror.

Even if I used every penny for a therapist, the memories might fade, and I might acquire tools to manage them when they came roaring to the surface of my consciousness, but I'd never be able to wipe them out completely.

"You're deep in thought tonight." Stuart held his hand out to me.

I hadn't even noticed the waiter bring the check or Stuart paying it.

"I'm tired. Sam had a rough night, so I got up early to give Ava a break."

Stuart smiled. He always did when I talked about my nephew. On our second date, he'd told me how much he loved kids and wanted to have a houseful.

I liked kids too, especially since my nephew was born. Prior to that, I'd never been around a baby. Sam was work, no doubt about that, but the joy he brought to my life was worth every dirty diaper I changed and every step I took pacing the floor in an attempt to get him to settle down and stop crying.

"Will you be warm enough if we walk back?" Stuart took off his jacket and put it around my shoulders.

I really didn't need his since I was wearing my own down jacket, but Stuart was a gentleman. It was one of the things I'd liked most about him when we first met.

I liked the feel of his arm around my shoulders as we walked back down the trail. It was comforting to be by his side. That's what I should be focusing on rather than comparing him to Striker. They were two very different men, and those differences were neither good nor bad.

I slipped Stuart's jacket off my shoulders when we got to my front door.

"Would you like to come in?" I put my hand over my mouth to stifle a yawn.

"Not tonight. You're tired."

Stuart leaned forward and kissed me goodnight. It was chaste like the others he gave me after every one of our dates. Every so often, things would heat up between us, but even then, it was never as scorching as it had been between Striker and me.

Stuart and I had been seeing each other for several weeks, and besides the occasional make-out session, he hadn't pushed for anything more. It was another thing he'd told me when we first began dating. He was as old-fashioned as he was gentlemanly. He believed in taking things slow, not rushing into a physical relationship before we got to know each other.

"I believe making love should be just that," he'd said. "Without love, it's just sex, and I have no interest in that."

It hadn't bothered me. If anything, it was a relief. In hindsight, my relationship with Striker had gotten physical far faster than it should have. As much as he'd reassured me otherwise, I still wondered if my lack of sexual experience was one of the reasons he'd ended things between us.

I watched Stuart pull his truck out of the driveway and drive away. As tired as I was, I doubted I'd sleep. Instead, I walked through the house and out onto the deck. Whether the weather was warm or cold like tonight, I tried to end as many days as I could looking out at the ocean.

It calmed me, gave me a sense of peace like nowhere else I'd ever lived. Maybe my mother was right about the money being compensation for my father's evil deeds. It had paid for the house I never would've been able to afford otherwise.

I closed my eyes, settling my mind on the sound of the waves crashing on the shore. That, and the smell of the sea, soothed me like a glass of warm milk did for my mother when she couldn't sleep.

When I opened my eyes and turned my head, I saw Striker standing on the trail with his hands in his pockets. Was my imagination playing tricks on me? How many times had I wished that the person knocking on my door was him instead of Stuart?

Striker walked closer.

"Where's the plumber?" he asked.

"He went home. How did you know...never mind."

"Word gets around."

"Do you want to come up on the deck?"

"Were you getting ready to go inside?"

"Not yet. I like to spend a few minutes out here before I go to sleep."

Striker climbed the steps. "Does this work?" he asked, pointing to the gas fire pit that sat in the center of several chairs.

"It does." I flipped the switch that ignited the flame.

"You don't mind, do you?"

"Not at all." I sat in one of the chairs and pulled the blanket I'd brought outside over me. "Are you warm enough?"

Striker nodded, holding his hands closer to the fire. "I think so, although I might just be numb."

"It's colder here than people think."

"It's the ocean." He looked out at it and then back at me. "You like it here."

"I do, and it's more than because Ava is here. I'd want to live here anyway."

"You're making a life for yourself."

"I guess, but lately it's felt pretty small."

"What? This town or your life?"

"My life."

"Are you still thinking about going back to school?"

"I'm not sure. I mean, to get the kind of job we've discussed in the past, I'd have to get my Ph.D."

"What's stopping you?"

"Time. Sam."

"Your nephew?"

I nodded.

"What about the University of Oregon?"

"I looked into their Neuroscience Program."

"They have a good reputation for their Behavioral Analysis programs."

"Griffin…never mind."

"What were you going to say?"

"It isn't important."

"It is to me."

I stood and flipped the switch to turn off the fire. "It's getting late."

"You're angry."

I clenched my fists inside my jacket pockets, turned back toward the ocean, and closed my eyes.

"Why do you know so much about the University of Oregon's neuroscience program?" I opened my eyes and went inside without waiting for his answer. I locked the slider, went straight into the bedroom, and threw myself on the bed.

We'd talked about my field of study several times and that if I were to continue my education, it would be with an emphasis on psychology and behavioral analysis. He'd even mentioned once that if I did choose that course of study, I might make an excellent profiler.

We'd never gotten far enough into it to talk about which schools I might apply to, which meant Striker would have had to look into the U of O on his own. But why would he spend the time on something like that if he didn't want me in his life?

7

Striker

I knew better than to do what I'd just done to Aine. I'd let her know I was keeping tabs on her, which I had no right to do.

Walking the trail from the hotel to her house had been wrong. Accepting her invitation to join her on the deck was foolish. I shouldn't be insinuating myself back into the life I'd walked out of so abruptly.

It had been eight months since I told her we needed to talk. Eight months since I stood back and watched her sadness turn to humiliation when I refused to tell her the real reason we couldn't continue seeing each other.

Aine had taken the blame for the relationship's demise squarely on her shoulders, and I'd done nothing to dissuade or reassure her. The angrier she was at me, the better, I'd thought at the time. If she hated me, never wanted to see me again, maybe I could force myself to stay away.

Now I'd done the very thing I knew then that I couldn't do. In the span of only a few seconds, I'd given her hope. Thankfully, her anger came to the surface quickly and she'd stormed away from me, saving us both the embarrassment.

I took my time walking back to the hotel. The exhaustion I'd felt earlier had faded away, leaving me with what I knew would be another sleepless night.

When the sun rose, I was still awake, staring out at the same ocean I'd been watching since I sat on the deck with Aine the night before.

I hadn't talked myself in or out of anything in the hours in between. I still knew I wasn't good for her, and yet I also still knew that as long as I was in Yachats, I wouldn't be able to resist talking to her, wanting to be around her, hearing her voice, and seeing her smile.

After the K19 meeting, I planned to get a flight out as soon as possible, even if it meant flying commercial, which I'd never minded doing. In fact, there were times I preferred it, especially if the rest of the team took a private plane.

The meeting today wasn't until zero eight hundred hours, which meant I had two hours to shower, get coffee, and check my email to see if McTiernan had anything else to report on Abdul Ghafor's whereabouts.

Whether he did or not, I had no intention of telling him what I knew or what I'd seen in Razor's office yesterday. The CIA couldn't be trusted to do the right thing where Ghafor was concerned. The K19 team, I knew, would do whatever it took to neutralize the bastard.

When I walked into the conference room where Ranger texted we'd be meeting, I surveyed those in attendance. Doc was there with his wife, Merrigan. Razor, Monk, Onyx, Ranger, and Diesel were there too.

Missing were Gunner and Mercer, aka Eighty-eight, the two other founding partners, along with Mantis, Alegria, and Dutch. Maybe Doc would give a rundown of why those missing weren't here.

The first person I greeted was Merrigan. Back when the two of us were starting our careers, me with the CIA and her with MI6, we'd had a brief affair. It was hard to imagine now, since I thought of her more like a sister than even a colleague.

"How are you, Striker?" she asked, kissing one cheek and then the other.

I pulled back and studied her. "Nowhere near as good as you are, by the looks of it."

Merrigan smiled. "I'm a very happy woman. I suppose it shows."

"It looks good on you," I said, turning to shake Doc's hand when he approached. "By the way, why are we meeting here?"

"That's my fault," answered Merrigan without elaborating.

"We had a few days on our own," explained Doc; Merrigan blushed. "We turned our trip here into a mini-vacation."

Not wanting to hear more, I excused myself and went to the breakfast buffet. I filled a plate and sat in the open seat next to Monk—assuring myself a quiet meal.

As I'd hoped, Doc started out by saying that given Gunner and Zary's baby, a little girl they'd named Lia Orina, was only three months old, Gunner sent his regrets for missing the meeting.

"Mantis and Alegria's baby boy was born last Tuesday. They named Ian after Mantis' brother who, we all know, was killed on September 11."

It didn't matter that neither was at the meeting; the group applauded anyway.

Doc added that Mercer, who was married to Doc's daughter, would be joining us at the next stage of the mission, which we were about to discuss, and finally, that Dutch was also on a leave of absence.

"I'm happy to report that both Ranger and Diesel have signed contracts with K19 Security Solutions, and while she isn't here presently, Corazón has also signed a pilot contract."

Doc looked at Onyx, who smiled and nodded. I wondered if he was happy to have an additional pilot on board, or if it was more that the pilot was a woman he'd been linked with romantically.

"What's the status of Tackle's and Halo's offers?" asked Razor.

Doc looked at Merrigan. "They've been extended, and I'm waiting to hear back. We decided it was premature for them to attend this meeting."

I was glad Razor had asked. Both Landry "Tackle" Sorenson and Knox "Halo" Clarkson had been part of my team since they joined the CIA. They were good men whom I still worked with occasionally as private contractors.

"Anyone else we should be discussing?" asked Razor, smirking.

"Not yet, asshole," answered Doc, shooting a look back at him.

That spiked my curiosity. "Who else, Doc?"

"Copeland."

I felt my blood pressure spike. Money McTiernan was Copeland's boss at the CIA. It was bad enough that we were considering making Cope an offer. If K19 extended one to McTiernan, I'd resign, effective immediately.

"Shouldn't this be something the partners agree on prior to offers being extended?"

"I'll answer," said Merrigan. "Striker, I would agree if we were extending partnerships, but we aren't any longer. The four men and one woman have all received offers of employment. As the managing partner, I make those decisions."

"Understood," I muttered. Later, I'd ask her about McTiernan, rather than putting her on the spot now. If she said they were considering making the man any kind of offer, I'd walk.

"Anything else on team members?" asked Doc, looking around the room. "Moving on, our next topic of discussion should raise the heat level in the room—Abdul Ghafor."

I had plenty to say on the subject, but I had no intention of doing so. I'd much rather get everyone else's take on it first.

"We've confirmed he's in Pakistan and that he's stockpiling weapons," said Razor.

"What about feet on the ground?" Doc asked.

"That's the thing. There's very little sign of soldiers."

"Weapons mean money," said Monk.

"Shit," said Razor, clutching his chest. "Raise your damn hand or something when you do that."

"What?"

"Talk."

Monk flipped him off and then looked at me. In fact, everyone was looking at me.

"What?" I asked, like Monk had.

"Fill us in," said Doc, sitting down next to Merrigan as if he was settling in for the remainder of the meeting. "Where's the money coming from?"

"I'd say that's obvious."

Doc motioned for me to stand.

"Look, it's no secret that I vehemently disagreed with the CIA's decision to exile Ghafor to Colombia. I have little doubt that the money is coming directly from the Islamic fundamentalists who have taken a stronghold in Buenaventura."

"Led by whom?" asked Merrigan.

"They're doing a damn good job keeping that a secret."

Razor had his laptop open and was scratching his chin. "Let's reopen dialogue with the Cuban."

I nodded. In March of the previous year, a Cuban national had been arrested in Bogotá for an alleged "terror plot" to kill American diplomats on behalf of Islamic State extremists. The plan had been for the man to blow himself up inside a restaurant popular with US Embassy staff and other foreigners in the *Zona Rosa* region of the city. K19 had played an integral role in neutralizing him before he could put his plan in action.

"Is he still alive?" asked Razor, still staring at his computer screen.

"To the best of my knowledge, although I doubt for long. Colombian officials amassed a trove of evidence against him."

From the seized cell phones, the Columbians learned that the Cuban had been calling and sending encrypted text messages to at least three other terror cell members in Morocco and Spain in the weeks leading up to his arrest. From what I understood, those suspects hadn't yet been located.

"It's your mission, Ellis. What do you do?" asked Doc.

"Hypothetically?"

"Not necessarily."

I put my hands on the table in front of me. "What I'd want to do is assassinate the bastard. However, in doing so, I'd lose the money trail along with his connections to the terror plot in Bogotá, as well as the lesser knowns."

"First phase?" asked Razor.

"We watch. Concurrently, we get someone on the money." The words were out of my mouth before I realized I'd been set up. "Fuck."

"Don't make any assumptions just yet. Eighty-eight is damn good at tracking financials," said Razor.

Mercer Bryant, or Eighty-eight as Razor had called him, was renowned for his forensic accounting abilities.

"You mentioned at the beginning of this meeting that he'd join us for phase two of the mission we would be discussing. Is this the mission?"

"Affirmative," answered Doc.

"What's phase one?"

"That's up to you, to a certain extent anyway. Let's nail down the basics. While Razor has a badass new setup here, the logistics of keeping everyone in Oregon are a nightmare. Therefore, I propose we work out of what is quickly becoming K19's Central Coast headquarters."

"Do we have any other headquarters I'm unaware of?" Razor asked.

"No, but at the rate we're growing, we're going to need to think about that," answered Merrigan.

I was all for moving the base of this operation down to California. Today, if possible. As far as other bases of operations, Ranger, Diesel, and I were all East Coasters, as were Tackle and Halo. Dutch was living in South Carolina, and Onyx was from the Southeast too. Maybe K19 should consider a setup in Virginia.

"Back to phase one," said Razor, looking at me.

"We watch. We'll know when to make a move."

"Copy that." Razor stood, picked up his computer, and walked over to where I was seated. "We're teaming up on this one," he said. "But it's your mission. I'm number two."

"Who else is on our team?"

"Your call, but for the time being, I say we put everyone on standby. Between the two of us, Monk, and Eighty-eight, we can handle monitoring the surveillance. If anything changes, it's easy enough to call in the cavalry."

"Agreed." If that was the plan, we didn't necessarily need to leave Yachats, but I didn't point that out. If only for my sanity, I needed to separate myself from Aine McNamara and the life she was making without me.

8

Aine

"How long will you be in California?" I asked Ava, who had just told me they'd be leaving in the morning.

"At least through Thanksgiving. Maybe longer."

Our mother wouldn't be back from her month-long cruise until the middle of December, and now Ava was leaving too and taking Sam with her.

What would I do with myself? Maybe I could start looking into the program at Oregon University Striker and I had talked about the night before.

I shook my head. What was I doing? We hadn't talked; he'd dropped a handful of bombs designed to make sure I was aware that he knew what was happening in my life, including my relationship with Stuart.

"You're going too," said Ava.

"What do you mean?" I bent down to pet Dasher, the dog Tabon had given Ava for Christmas.

"You aren't going to stay here alone."

"Why not?"

"Aine, come on. Be serious. Can you really be away from your nephew for an indefinite amount of time?"

"It didn't sound like I was invited."

Ava set a handful of diapers on the bed. "You're *always* invited."

"I wouldn't make such a blanket statement if I were you. Tabon might not appreciate having his sister-in-law in tow everywhere you go."

Ava shook her head. "He loves you."

"Loving me and wanting me to be a constant in your lives are two different things."

"Wait until he gets back. I'll let him convince you."

We both headed toward the nursery when we heard Sam wail through the baby monitor.

"You can get him," said Ava, holding back.

"No, he's your son. I'm sorry."

Ava folded her arms. "I'm not being noble. I have a lot to do."

I smiled and raced off to pluck my nephew from the crib. "Hello, sweet boy," I said, lifting him into my arms. "Did you have a good nap?"

Sam was the most beautiful baby I'd ever seen. He had his father's jet-black hair and blue eyes like Ava and I had. At his last appointment, the doctor had told Ava and Razor that Sam was in the ninety-eighth percentile of both height and weight, which Tabon said was because my sister produced more milk than any mother in the history of the universe.

Ava had swatted at him when he said it, and pretended to pout. When Tabon had put his arms around her and nuzzled her neck, I left.

I didn't begrudge Ava any happiness, but there were times I was envious. Tabon more than loved Ava; he worshiped her, and she felt the same way about him. I'd foolishly thought Striker might feel the same way about me. How stupid I'd been.

"Do you want to feed him, or should I grab a bottle from downstairs?" I asked. Ava pumped enough milk every day that Sam could probably get by with nothing but bottles for at least a week.

"I have to keep packing so go ahead."

"Hey," I said to Tabon when he walked in and found me sitting on the sofa, feeding his son.

"There's my boy." He ran his finger down Sam's cheek.

"Can I ask you something?"

"Always."

"Do you get tired of me being around all the time?"

Tabon sat on the coffee table in front of me, leaned forward, and put his elbows on his knees.

"What's this all about?" he asked.

"Just that. I'm always here. Maybe you'd like to come home and not find your wife's sister in your house."

"You're not here all the time, Aine. If anything, I worry that Avarie and I are always imposing on you. I doubt you signed up to be a full-time nanny when your sister had this big guy."

Sam reached for his father, and Tabon took him in his arms.

"Ava said you're leaving for California."

He looked at me but didn't say anything right away.

"What?" I asked when he continued staring.

"I'm not sure what I'm supposed to say."

"Oh." I scooted forward on the sofa to stand; Tabon put his hand on my arm.

"I know I just said that I feel like we're always imposing on you, but I'm not sure your sister will want to go along if you don't come too."

"Won't I be the imposition, though? I'll go from being underfoot most of the time, to all of the time if I'm staying with you."

Razor nipped at Sam's hand when the baby put it near his mouth, and he giggled.

"There's another solution."

"What's that?"

"You can stay in Gunner's half of the duplex. He and Zary won't be coming out between now and the first of the year, and maybe by then, either you'll be sick of us and want to come back home, or we'll all come home."

"Are you sure? It seems kind of big for just me."

"Not an issue. You'll have loads of privacy, and Ava will have you close. Your mom's on a cruise, right?"

"If you're sure..."

"Positive."

"I have one question, though."

"Shoot."

"Will Striker be there?"

"If by 'there' you mean at the house, maybe sometimes, but he definitely won't be staying there. We haven't figured out the logistics yet, but he'll either be at the safe house in Harmony or down in Montecito, closer to Doc's place."

"Okay."

"What happened with you two? If you don't want to tell me, I'll understand."

"I think he got bored."

Tabon raised his eyebrows. "Not a chance. Maybe he just got scared."

"Of me? That's hysterical."

Razor shrugged. "I bet I'm more right than you are."

One thing about being around Tabon and the rest of the K19 team that always astounded me was how many vehicles they had.

When I asked about driving my car down from Yachats, he scoffed.

"There's one in the garage you can use."

"What about when you need it?"

"No, I meant in Gunner's garage. Avarie and I both have cars in Cambria."

"You do?"

He nodded and went back to what he was doing.

"I don't know how he's getting there, but Tabon said that Striker—I mean Griffin—wouldn't be on the plane today," said Ava when we were getting ready to leave for the private airfield.

"It's okay. You can call him Striker. I do now." I'd felt funny calling him by his code name when we were dating, but now that we weren't, there was no reason I shouldn't refer to him the same way everyone else did.

Tabon walked past us, carrying our bags. "Striker left last night."

I was equally relieved and disappointed. A part of me had hoped he'd be on the plane, whether he talked to me or not.

"What's happening with Stuart?" Tabon asked when he came back inside after putting the bags in the car.

"I talked to him last night. He's going to try to take a couple of days off to come down to visit. If that's okay. I mean, he wouldn't stay at the house or anything like that."

Tabon put his hand on my shoulder. "You're my sister-in-law, not my daughter. You don't need my permission to have guests. Even overnight ones. You have the run of that side of the duplex, sweetheart. The only thing I ask is that if you have loud parties, you invite your sister and me."

"Right." I laughed. "As if."

"I don't know," said Ava. "Quinn's back."

And I couldn't wait to see her. Quinn was the reason that Ava met Tabon, which led to me meeting Striker.

"Do you think it'll be too hard for her, you know, with Sam?"

It had been over a year since we'd seen Quinn and her husband, Mercer. The last time they were in town had been for Ava and Tabon's wedding. Quinn was pregnant at the time but had miscarried a couple of weeks after that. Since, she and Mercer had been traveling around the world.

"When I asked him if he'd take me to India, Mercer said he'll take me everywhere," Quinn had gushed shortly after she and Mercer started seeing each other.

He'd made good on his promise, and they'd spent the last year going everywhere from Europe to the Caribbean—even to places I'd never heard of.

"I wish Tara and Penelope could come for Thanksgiving," said Ava, looking sheepishly over her shoulder at Tabon.

He shook his head and kissed her. "Then, invite them, Avarie. Aine was saying the duplex was too big for just her."

"What do you think?" asked Ava.

"We should definitely invite them. It's been too long since the Tribe of Five was all in the same place at the same time."

We'd met in boarding school when we were seven years old—and had been best friends since. It was only after we graduated from Barnard that we'd lived separate lives.

From the beginning, the thing we had in common was that each of us had not-so-great relationships with our parents.

When we were younger, we'd collectively decided Quinn had it the worst. After she arrived at boarding school, she and her mother saw each other so sporadically that there were times it seemed like Quinn didn't have any parents at all.

She didn't find out who her dad was until she was twenty-one years old, and even then there had been some question as to whether Doc was her biological father. The night before her wedding to Mercer, Quinn and Doc opened the envelope that confirmed he was.

While Quinn's story had a happy ending, Ava's and mine didn't. Shortly after the very same wedding, we found out our father, who had lived his life with us as Conor McNamara, was actually Makar Petrov, a black-market arms dealer. Over the course of the next several months, he'd tried to kill Ava, me, and our half sister, Zary, in order to get his hands on money he'd put in our names when we were born.

I shuddered. There was no reason to dredge up those memories. The nightmare began with the man we'd once called "Daddy," and still hadn't ended even though he was dead.

Tara and Penelope had lousy relationships with their parents too, but nothing as dramatic as what Ava, Quinn, or I had gone through. For them, it was the stereotypical scenario of their fathers turning in their "older wives" for newer models every couple of years while their mothers were angry and bitter about it.

Regardless of the situation, it was rare any of us spent holidays with our families.

"I'll send an email on our way to the airfield," I offered.

Maybe if the Tribe of Five was back together again, they could help me get my mind off Striker Ellis.

9

Striker

I'd sprung for a first-class ticket even though it was a quick flight from Portland to the Central Coast. Originally, I'd planned to leave last night, but decided to stay in the city instead. I spent three hours going from shops to restaurants to other shops, eating my way through downtown and buying gifts with no intended recipient. Each thing I'd picked out was because I thought Aine might like it—even though I obviously couldn't give them to her.

It wasn't as though I could give any of my purchases to someone in my family either. The first week of March, I'd received word that my last living relative had died.

My sister, Pam, had battled drugs and alcohol all her short life, until one day, her body had simply given out.

As for my parents, my mother left home when I was in kindergarten. I barely remembered her. Three years later, my father skipped town and left me and my sister all alone. My mother's only sibling, Dorothy, took the two of us in. I was eight at the time. My sister was fifteen and had no intention of living by our aunt's strict rules.

Looking back on it, Dorothy hadn't been that strict. The rules she made were reasonable. It was just that my parents hadn't lived their own lives with any self-discipline that would provide stability for their kids.

When my aunt passed away, I was the only one at the cemetery on the day she was buried. I realized then that I was alone. For all intents and purposes, I had no family left—they'd all abandoned me.

A few weeks later, a woman claiming to be my mother had shown up at the CIA headquarters, high on drugs and demanding her share of whatever I'd inherited from Dorothy. When I informed her that there wasn't any inheritance, she told me to expect to hear from her lawyer.

I did eventually hear from an attorney, but not about any inheritance. Instead, the man had been attempting to collect past-due medical bills on behalf of my now-deceased mother. When I suggested the man look for her husband instead, he said that he did and had found he had passed away a few months before her. That was how I found out both of my parents were dead. One phone call. From a lawyer looking for money.

I reached into my pocket and pulled out the sheer bag that held the delicate pair of garnet earrings I purchased because they matched the bracelet I gave to Aine at Christmas, the one that had belonged to my aunt,

Dorothy. Aine had tried to return it when I broke things off with her.

It wasn't the phone call from the lawyer looking for money for my mother's medical bills that made me end our relationship, though. It was what I learned from the one I received informing me of my sister's death.

I closed my eyes against the memory of what had turned out to be one of the worst days of my life.

***

Aine came into the kitchen, poured a cup of coffee, and joined me at the table.

"Is everything okay?" she asked, opening the door for me to act sooner than I'd planned to.

"It isn't."

When she reached across the table to put her hand on mine, I pulled it away.

"Griffin?"

"This isn't going to work out, Aine."

"What do you mean?"

"You and me. We've run our course."

I'd expected her look of confusion and maybe some tears, but so far, she wasn't crying.

"I don't understand."

"We talked about the age difference between us in the past, and it's more of an issue than I thought it would be."

Her cheeks turned bright red. "I see."

"We have very different lives. It isn't only that I'm so much older than you are. I have a career, and I know what I want out of life. I thought I wanted a long-term relationship, but I've realized I don't. I tried, and it isn't what I thought it would be."

There was little she could say in argument, and I'd planned it that way.

She rose from the table and walked toward the bedroom; I didn't follow. If I did, I might be tempted to take back everything I said and tell her the real reason I was ending things between us. I couldn't do that, though. I could feel my heart splinter, but my pain didn't matter. I couldn't saddle someone like Aine with the baggage I'd be carrying with me the rest of my life.

She rolled her small suitcase into the kitchen and told me she'd called a car service to pick her up.

"I can give you a ride, Aine."

"No, thank you. I'll wait outside."

"Aine—"

"Please, Griffin. You said what you needed to say. I'd rather not discuss it further." She opened the door and walked out. Again, I didn't follow.

***

I put the earrings back in my pocket, telling myself I needed to stop the foolishness of buying gifts for a woman who was no longer in my life, but knowing full well that the next time I saw something I thought she would like, I wouldn't be able to resist.

As hard as it was to leave Yachats without seeing her one more time, it was for the best. I'd angered her when I made it obvious I thought about her, even paid attention to her life. She would never know the real extent to which I did.

"Were those earrings for your wife?" the older woman sitting in the seat next to me asked.

"Just a friend."

"She's a lucky woman."

"She wouldn't agree."

The woman touched my arm. "Why wouldn't she?"

Much to my surprise, I found myself telling the woman about Aine and our history.

"I did what I thought was best for her," I admitted, "but I miss her every day."

The woman studied me with her chin in her hand.

"I feel like there's something you want to say."

She raised and lowered her eyebrows with the deep breath she took and then patted my hand. "You don't need to hear my opinion to know what you need to do next."

"If you're going to say anything other than I should stay away from her, I disagree."

"You can't stay away from her, and you know it. Even when you aren't with her physically, you carry her with you. You're never without this woman, yet you've forced her to live her life without you."

"It's for the best."

"No matter how many times you say it, you aren't convincing yourself any more than you're convincing me."

"I don't know..."

"Of course you do."

"She's seeing someone else now."

The woman shrugged. "In the words of a well-known Broadway actor and producer, 'love is love is love is love.' There's no denying love, young man." The woman shook her head. "For someone so obviously bright, you are quite dim when it comes to the female heart."

I was intrigued. "I've told you far more about me than her. What makes you think she loves me?"

"I'm a woman."

I laughed a second time. "And?"

"Please don't take this the wrong way—I am old enough to be your mother, as well as very happily married—but you're very lovable."

"If you knew me better, you wouldn't say that."

"Yes, I would, and so would your young lady. Ask her."

"I doubt I'll ever talk to her again."

This time the woman laughed. "Of course you will. Very soon, in fact."

"Are you psychic? Not that I believe in that sort of thing."

"Intuitive."

"She's still in Oregon."

When the pilot announced our descent, the woman closed her eyes and rested her head against her seat.

I didn't add anything more until after we landed and separated at the gate.

"Enjoy your stay," I said, not knowing whether she was visiting or coming home.

"Follow your heart, young man." She waved before walking in the opposite direction.

Her words stuck with me the rest of the day. The cynic in me knew they were nonsense, spoken by a woman who knew very little about the reality of the situation. There was another part of me that wished, even hoped, she was right.

10

Aine

"Striker is on his way here now," said Tabon, looking at his phone.

"Oh. I guess that means I should leave."

"I didn't say that. I just said he's on his way."

"You don't have to hide from him, Aine. You didn't do anything wrong and neither did he. You broke up. That's it. You're both adults who can learn to be around each other."

I wanted to slap the condescension seeping from my sister right off her face. If the situations were reversed, Ava wouldn't have even agreed to come to California. It was easy for her to lecture, now that she was happily married.

"Whatever," I said under my breath.

"Don't leave in a huff," Ava said, following me to the front door.

"I'll come back later." I closed the door in her face and then looked up when I heard the sound of the electric front gate opening. As much as I wished I could, there was no way to get down the steps and into the other front door before Striker saw me. Instead, I took a deep breath and waited while he parked.

"Hi," I said when he got out of the car and walked toward me.

"Hi." He smiled and shook his head.

My shoulders tightened. Was he laughing at me? I turned away.

"Wait," I heard him say before he touched my arm. "Someone told me I was going to see you sooner than I thought I would, and they were right. That's why I smiled."

I folded my arms, not knowing how to respond.

"This isn't easy for either of us, Aine, but I'd really like it if we could be friends."

"You've got to be kidding."

"I'm sorry about the way our last conversation ended."

What could I say? My only regret was that we'd talked at all.

"Aine?"

"What, Striker?"

He raised his eyebrows. I'd only ever called him Griffin. "I mean it. I want to be your friend."

"I can't do this."

When he reached out to touch my arm a second time, I shrugged away and punched the code into the keypad on the door. It clicked and I went inside, forcing myself not to look back. If I did, I'd say something I'd regret, or worse, throw my arms around him and beg him to take me back.

I leaned against the closed door and took a deep breath. Could I do this, or should I get on the next plane back to Oregon?

After thirty minutes, I decided my sister was right; I was behaving like an adolescent.

"Hey," I said, walking back into the kitchen where Ava was feeding Sam.

"Uh, hi."

"You were right. Striker and I dated, and now we're not, and I need to get over it."

Ava raised a brow.

"Don't. Just accept that I intend to fake it until I make it, and I could use your support."

"You've got it." Ava set the spoon down on the counter out of Sam's reach and hugged me. "Sorry about the tough love."

"I needed to hear it."

"Want to take Sam into town and do some shopping?"

"Absolutely." I loved the shops and restaurants in the seaside village. "Maybe we could have lunch too."

"I'll go tell Tabon." Ava took Sam out of the high chair and handed him to me.

"Hey, big boy," I said, kissing his cheek. Sam rested his head on my shoulder and a sense of calm washed over me. I never dreamed I could love someone as much as I loved him.

"Striker is downstairs," said Ava when she came back up.

"I saw him."

"Oh."

"It was fine, Ava. Like you said, no big deal." It actually had been a big deal, but I had no intention of admitting it.

Ava touched the tip of Sam's nose with her finger. "Ready to go shopping?"

Sam smiled and reached for his mother.

I followed them out to the car, wondering if Striker would still be at the house when we got back.

The village of Cambria was separated into two parts by a long block of open space. Ava suggested we spend the morning on the north side, have lunch, and then spend the afternoon in the southern part of town.

"We should stop by Stave and pick up a bottle of wine before we go back to the house later," she suggested.

"Good idea," I answered.

"Don't forget Christmas is a little over a month away," Ava reminded me when I took full advantage of lavishing presents on Sam at both the bookshop and toy store. "You could save some of these gifts and give them to him then."

"Or I could come back and buy more."

Ava smiled and shook her head. "You're going to spoil him."

"That's the idea."

By the time we came out of the kitchen-gadget store, I was starving. "Can we eat at the place next door to the garden shop?"

Ava nodded. "It isn't Tabon's favorite, because it's strictly vegetarian, so I'd love it."

We sat on the outdoor patio since there were heat lamps, so we could enjoy the restaurant's lush gardens.

"I want to plant a vegetable garden this year," said Ava.

"Where?"

"Good question. I'm not sure how long we'll be in California."

"Do you think you'll be here for Christmas?"

"You say that as though you won't be."

"I didn't plan to be gone that long."

"But...never mind."

"Say it, Ava."

"No offense, but it isn't like you have anything to get back to."

"How nice. I guess you've forgotten that I have a boyfriend."

"Is that the only reason you'd go back?"

"Ava, I do have a life of my own."

The look on Ava's face mirrored my insecurities. Outside of dating Stuart, I didn't do much other than spend time with her and Sam.

"I'm going back to school."

"Why?"

"Because I want to."

"But you hated school."

"Actually, I didn't. You did."

"Yeah, that sounds right. Where would you go?"

"The University of Oregon has a Neuroscience and Behavior graduate program. If I wanted to, I could get my Ph.D. there too."

"Isn't the university over two hours from Yachats?"

"Ava, as you said, I don't have anything 'to get back to.' It's time I had a life of my own."

"You couldn't commute that far every day."

I sighed. "No, but I could come home on the weekends."

Ava looked over at Sam, sound asleep in his stroller.

"Your nephew will miss you."

"He's four months old, Ava. He doesn't know whether I'm around every day or not."

"I do."

"There will come a time when I don't live next door to you. Maybe you should start preparing yourself now." I smiled, but Ava didn't.

"Why did Striker break up with you?"

"Whoa. How did me saying I won't live next to you all our lives segue into my ex-boyfriend breaking up with me?"

"You never said why."

"I was too immature and inexperienced for him. Part of it was that I didn't have a life of my own."

"He said that?"

"Not those exact words, but he said his life was 'established' and mine wasn't."

"That's a pretty shitty thing to say. Your life has been in turmoil since we graduated from college. Both of our lives have been."

"It hasn't stopped you."

Ava rested her elbows on the table. “I married my *bodyguard*, Aine. Let that roll around in your head for a couple of minutes.”

I laughed when Ava did. That much was true. My sister’s relationship with her husband had started out with him protecting her.

“Quinn did too,” Ava added, still laughing.

“I hadn’t thought of it that way. Well, see, I never had a bodyguard, so I guess I’ll be single forever.”

“What about Stuart?”

“You mean what about marrying him?”

Ava nodded and I shrugged. “It’s too early in the relationship for me to think about that.”

“You wouldn’t marry him, though, would you?”

“I just said it’s too soon for me to think about it.”

“But you would’ve married Striker.”

“Stop it, Ava.”

“All I’m saying is that you were willing to marry Striker—”

“No, I wasn’t.”

“Let me finish. It didn’t work out with Striker, but you *could* marry Stuart.”

I stood and threw my napkin on the table. “Thanks, Ava. I’m twenty-three years old, and my own sister is suggesting that I better latch on to the guy who *might* be willing to marry me. Way to make me feel even worse about myself."

"That wasn't my intention."

"Whether it was or not, you succeeded." I reached into my purse and pulled out enough money to cover the entire check.

"What are you doing?"

"I'm paying for lunch, and I'm leaving."

"You're overreacting."

"Just because I let you get away with saying something like that once today, doesn't mean I'm going to allow you to keep doing it. I'm entitled to my feelings, Ava."

"Are you seriously leaving?"

"Yep. As a matter of fact, it's time for me to go back to Oregon."

I stormed out of the restaurant and through the parking lot, to the trail I knew led back to Moonstone Beach. The two-mile walk would give me time to think things over, although I doubted I'd change my mind about leaving.

My sister needed to learn it wasn't okay for her to tell me everything she disapproved of. I was sick of hearing how perfect Ava's life was compared to mine.

Little Miss Judgy could keep her condescending comments to herself since I wouldn't be around to listen.

I wasn't surprised to see Ava's car in the open garage when I walked up to the duplex, but I was that my sister wasn't outside, waiting for me.

I punched the code into the keypad and opened the front door when the lock clicked. I was almost done packing my stuff when I heard a knock.

I stalked toward the door and flung it open, ready to tell Ava everything on my mind, but it wasn't my sister standing on the other side of the threshold; it was Striker.

"Can I come in?"

"I'm in the middle of something."

"I know."

"What do you mean you know?"

"Ava told me you two had an argument."

"Interesting. First my sister doesn't have enough respect for me to let me live my life the way I want to. Now she doesn't have respect for my privacy either."

"In her defense—"

"Spare me," I said, attempting to shut the door in his face, but he put his arm out too quickly.

"She was crying, and when Razor pushed her to tell him why, I overheard."

"I get it. The bad twin hurt the good twin's feelings." I rolled my eyes and folded my arms. "I need to pack. I'm going home."

"I wish you wouldn't."

"You don't get a say in this."

He ran his hand through his hair. "I know I don't have any right to even be talking to you, but I'm going to say what I came over here to tell you anyway."

"Don't bother."

When I stalked into the bedroom, Striker followed.

"Once you get back to Yachats, you're going to wish you hadn't left so abruptly. You're going to feel sorry about your argument with Ava, but your pride won't let you get on a plane and come back."

There were countless things I wanted to say in response, but he was right. That was exactly how I'd feel. Instead of being vindicated, I'd be lonely and filled with regret, but unable to force myself to say I was sorry and come back.

"Give it some time. If you're still angry tomorrow, leave."

I didn't know why Striker was here, why I was listening to him, or why, when he touched my cheek, I didn't pull away.

"I hate to think your anger is because of me."

"It isn't. I'm mad at my sister."

"My guess is because she said something about me."

"You may think you know everything, but you don't."

He grabbed my hand and looked at my wrist. "I know you're still wearing the bracelet I gave you for Christmas."

"Only to remind me to return it to you."

"I don't believe you." Striker put his hand in his pocket and pulled out a sheer blue bag. "I got these for you."

I shook my head. "*Why?*"

"I knew how nice they'd look with your bracelet."

"Griffin, you can't—"

"I like hearing you call me that far more than Striker. I want us to be friends, Aine. I want that so much."

"I don't." I refused to take the bag from his hand.

"You're angry. I get that. But I hope one day you won't be anymore, and you'll see that I only want the best for you." He held the bag out again. "Please accept these. Consider them a peace offering."

I wanted to take them, but I couldn't bring myself to. It was as wrong for me to accept gifts from him as it was for him to buy them.

"You should give them to someone else."

Striker tilted his head and smiled. "If you refuse to take them now, I'll hang on to them until you're ready."

"You broke up with me. People don't buy gifts for people they broke up with."

"Lots of people buy gifts for their friends."

"You shouldn't be one of them."

He looked at his watch. "I'm sorry, but I need to get back. Are you going to stick around?"

"I haven't decided yet."

"I hope you do."

My phone buzzed, and I looked at the screen. "I need to take this."

"Is it the plumber?"

"That's none of your business."

11

Striker

As I walked back to the other side of the house, I thought about the conversation I'd had with Razor earlier. "Before we get started, there's something I need to say."

"Yeah?"

"I want to talk about Aine."

Razor's eyes hooded, and by the look on his face, it wasn't a topic he wanted to broach.

"All I ask is that you hear me out."

When Razor nodded, I proceeded to tell him everything I'd told the woman on the plane.

"I told you a year ago that if you hurt Aine, I'd kill you," Razor said when I finished talking.

"Yeah, you did."

"You're still alive, which means I knew you must've had a damn good reason for ending things with her." Razor scratched his chin. "I don't think you're giving her enough credit, though."

"I'm sure if Aine knew the truth, she would tell me it doesn't matter, but Razor, it matters to me."

"How much of what you told her is true?"

I hadn't expected the question. "I don't know."

"The part about not wanting to be in a long-term relationship—was that the truth?"

"It doesn't matter. There are other reasons—"

Razor held up his hand. "I understand that, Striker. What I'm asking is if those other reasons didn't exist, would you have stayed with Aine? Made a life with her?"

"I don't know," I said for the second time.

I went downstairs and studied the monitor I had watched most of the morning, waiting to see what Ghafor would do next.

It appeared the shipments of arms had slowed, but I doubted they'd stop entirely. The amount of ammunition Abdul was stockpiling was alarming. If forced to, I'd make arrangements for the CIA to take him out along with the weapons stored on his compound.

I'd much rather that happened after we found out where Ghafor's stream of money flowed from, though, along with what he planned to do with all his newly acquired weapons of mass destruction.

"Is Aine really leaving?" Razor asked, walking back into the office.

"I think I talked her into staying."

Razor shook his head.

"What?"

"I may not have always been your biggest fan—"

"Thanks."

"Hear me out. You're good for Aine. I just wish things had gone differently."

I scowled. "Well, they didn't. Do you want to get back to work, or should we call it a day?"

Razor laughed. "I don't miss Gunner as much when you're around. Wanna know why not?"

"Not particularly."

"I'll tell you anyway. You're just ornery enough that you remind me of him."

I flipped him off and went back to tracking Ghafor's movements. It looked as though he was leaving the compound. Depending on where he went, this might be the break we needed in order to gain a better understanding of what he was up to.

12

Aine

"Hi, Tara," I said. "Did you get my message?"

"I did. Pen and I are so excited to visit. It seems like we haven't seen you and Ava in forever. I can't even remember what Quinn looks like. Have you seen her yet?"

"No, but she and Mercer are coming for dinner tonight."

"They aren't leaving on another world adventure soon, are they?"

I laughed. "I'll let you know if they are. When will you be here?"

"That's trickier now that Penelope has a job. She actually has to ask for time off."

"Don't sound so disgusted. Having a job is a good thing, Tara. When are you going to look for one?"

"That's rich, Miss Pot, when are you?"

"I'm going back to school."

Tara gasped. Evidently, that was worse than getting a job.

"You are such a snob."

"I am not. I just never thought you'd go back to school."

"Why not?"

"You don't need to worry about money, Aine. So why bother?"

"Because I think there's more to life than shopping?"

"Whatever. Let me know how Quinn is."

"Right."

I ended the call, wondering why I bothered talking to Tara. She was a judgmental bitch. I shook my head when I heard a knock at the door. If it was Striker again, I really wasn't in the mood to listen to another lecture. I looked through the peephole; this time it was Ava, whom I wasn't in the mood to talk to either.

"What?"

"Can I come in?"

"If you must." I waved her in.

"Tabon told me Striker told him you're not leaving."

"I never said that."

"Maybe it was a feeling he got."

"Whatever." I plopped down on the sofa.

"Are you?"

"Not until I see Quinn."

Ava sat on the sofa, next to me. "I'm sorry."

I didn't respond; I was still too angry.

"I don't understand why you and Striker broke up when it seems as though you both still care about each other."

"He wants to be friends. By the way, I talked to Tara. Pen has to check her work schedule before they can let us know when they'll arrive."

Ava nodded. "Aine, I wish you'd forgive me."

"And I wish you wouldn't talk to me like you're perfect. You're married. So what? If you weren't, you wouldn't know what you wanted to do with your life either."

"You're right."

"I don't want you to give me any more unsolicited advice about Striker. Not a word. Understand?"

"But if you ask, I can, right?"

"That's the difference between solicited and unsolicited."

"You don't have to be a bitch about it."

"Neither do you."

Ava stood. "I came over to apologize, but if you aren't going to accept it, I'll leave."

"Okay. I accept your apology."

Ava sat back down. "I need to get back anyway. Tabon is watching Sam, and I know he and Striker have work to do."

"Let me know when he leaves, and I'll come over."

Ava looked away.

"What?"

"Tabon invited him to dinner."

Great. Just great. Unless I wanted to hide out, I was going to be forced to spend time with him.

"What are you thinking?"

"I'm going for a run. I'll come over later."

Ava kissed my cheek and then walked to the front door. "Can I ask a favor?"

"What?"

"If I bring Dasher over, can you take her with you?"

"Sure."

I went into the bedroom, changed my clothes, and met Ava and the dog by the door. Dasher looked like a full-grown dog, but she still had the energy of a puppy. A run would do her as much good as it would me.

I led the dog down the pathway from the house to the beach. It was cold, so there was hardly anyone out, which suited me fine. Part of the reason I wanted to run was to get away from other humans. Dasher was okay, as long as she didn't start talking to me.

Once I got partway down the beach, I realized I wasn't going to be able to cross over the usually dry river bed since it was high tide, so I turned around and ran back. It meant my run was nowhere near as long as I'd wanted it to be, unless I ran on the road, which I didn't want to do with Dasher.

I stopped and picked up a piece of driftwood and threw it for the dog, who instead of bringing it back to me, dropped it in the water. So much for playing fetch.

When I took the pathway up to the house, Striker was standing in the backyard.

"How was your run?" he asked.

"Too short. I'm going to drive north and see if I can find a longer stretch of beach open."

"Mind if I come with you?"

What? Why? "I thought you were working."

"We're taking a break."

"I'm not sure how long I'll be gone, so—"

"I'm not on any kind of schedule. There's a twelve-hour difference between us and Pakistan, so there isn't much happening now."

I almost asked what they were working on in Pakistan, but stopped myself. One, he probably couldn't tell me, and two, I needed to stop thinking about what Striker was doing or thinking or feeling.

"Please."

I wanted to cry in frustration. "It isn't a good idea."

"Would the plumber be jealous of you going on a run with a friend?"

"We aren't friends."

"I've told you I want to be."

When I sat on the grass and Dasher climbed into my lap, Striker sat down too.

"You said the age difference between us was a bigger issue than you thought it would be. You said your life was set and I didn't have one."

He smiled. "I didn't say you didn't have a life."

"I'm not playing games, Griffin—I mean, Striker. Semantics don't matter. You know what you said as well as I do. Are you really going to argue with me if I don't repeat it verbatim?"

He frowned and looked out at the ocean. "No, I'm not."

"Why are you even talking to me?"

"Because I miss talking to you. We used to talk for hours, and I don't do that with anyone but you. I know I said a romantic relationship wouldn't work between us, but I didn't mean I never wanted to talk to you again."

"You went eight months without needing to talk to me."

"You aren't going to make this easy for me, are you?"

"You didn't make it easy for me. One day you were all in, and the next, it was over. You weren't even willing to talk about it. Now, you want to be friends." I shook my head and stood. "I have enough friends."

"Wait," he called out. Something in his voice made me stop and look back at him.

"Go ahead," I said when he just stared at me.

"This isn't easy for me to say."

"Just say it and get it over with."

"Even if we can't be friends, can we please not be enemies?"

Staring into his eyes, I recognized the pain reflected in them. I'd only seen it once before, and it was at Christmas when he gave me the bracelet that had belonged to his aunt.

"Did something happen?"

"What do you mean?"

"Did you lose someone close to you?"

When he looked away from me, I knew I was on the right track. I sat back down.

"What happened, Griffin?"

"How did you know?"

"I'm not sure. The look in your eyes, I guess."

"It was nothing I didn't expect, and my sister wasn't someone I was close to."

"I'm sorry."

"Don't be. I hadn't seen her in years, and even before then, we didn't have a relationship." He turned back and looked into my eyes. “Don’t pity me, Aine. That isn’t what this is about. I don’t want you to be my friend because you feel sorry for me.”

I put my hands on the grass behind me and leaned back. “I don’t pity you. I’m mad at you. It doesn’t mean I don’t like you anymore.”

“So, friends?”

“When did your sister pass away?”

“Earlier in the year.”

“When?”

“March.”

“Before you broke up with me?”

He looked away, nodded, and stood. “I better get back to work.”

“I thought you wanted to go for a run.”

“Maybe next time.”

I took Dasher inside and sent a text to Ava, asking her to come over.

Within five minutes, I heard a knock.

“It’s open,” I hollered.

“What’s up?” Ava asked.

“I just had the weirdest conversation with Striker.”

“What about?”

“He was telling me he wanted to be friends, and then he told me his sister died.”

“That is weird.”

"I haven't told you the weird part yet. I asked him when she died, and he said in March. Then when I asked if it was before we broke up, he said it was."

"Why didn't he tell you then?"

"That's what I think is so strange."

"Do you think it has anything to do with why he broke things off with you?"

"It's the only thing that makes sense to me."

"Again, why?"

"I don't know yet."

"But you're going to try to find out?"

"I know you'll think I'm crazy, but I fell in love with Striker. I never dreamed we'd break up."

"Why would I think that's crazy?"

"Because it was so quick."

"Not quicker than Tabon and me."

"You've got a point." I shook my head. "All this time, I've struggled with understanding why. Nothing he said at the time made any sense."

"Why would his sister's death make him end things, though?"

"Like I said, I don't know, but I intend to find out."

My phone vibrated, and I pulled it out of my back pocket. "I got a text from Quinn. They're on their way. We should go next door."

Ava touched my hand. "I know this is hard..."

"I'll be all right. I need to get my mind off Striker, anyway." I put a smile on my face and led Ava next door. "I'm so excited to see Quinn. I can't believe how long it's been."

Ava studied me once we were back in her kitchen. "It looks like Tabon opened a bottle of wine; would you like a glass?"

"I'd love one. Thanks."

Ava handed me the drink she'd just poured and then poured herself another.

"Cheers! To the Tribe of Five being back together very soon. Unless Mercer whisks Quinn away again."

"We can't let him. At least not until Pen and Tara get here."

I scowled.

"What's that look all about? I thought you were trying to get your mind off Striker."

"Not him, Tara."

"Uh-oh."

"She was giving me a hard time about going back to school."

Ava raised a brow.

"Who cares? Let's not talk about her. Let's drink wine."

"Sounds good to me," said Tabon, joining us in the kitchen. "Want a glass?" he asked when Striker came in too.

"Thanks, but I should hit the road."

"What? You're not going anywhere, mister," said Ava with hands on her hips. "You told me you were staying for dinner." My sister pointed to the dining table that was set for six.

"It's okay," I said. "If you need to go, go."

Striker looked into my eyes. "I guess I can stay."

"*They're here*!" shouted Ava, looking out the kitchen window.

Both Ava and I ran out the front door.

13

Striker

"Don't let Ava push you around. If you don't want to stay for dinner, you don't have to."

"If you'd rather not have me here—"

Razor gripped my shoulder. "Knock that shit off, Striker. Gunner isn't here, so you can relax, and know you're welcome."

I laughed and so did Razor. He was right, Gunner didn't keep his dislike of me a secret.

"Although, you won't get much of Aine's attention tonight. They haven't seen Quinn since our wedding."

It was hard to fathom everything that happened in that time. Aine and I met at that wedding, and in between, we'd fallen in love—at least I had—and broken up.

* * *

"This is a bad idea," I said to Monk as we walked through the beach house.

"You're part of the team."

"That doesn't mean Razor wants me at his wedding."

I was halfway down the steps to the beach when I saw *her.*

I recognized the woman. She was Ava McNamara's twin, Aine, and she took my breath away. With her tan skin, sandy-blonde hair, and curves that made my mouth water, she looked like the quintessential California girl. I knew better, though; she'd been raised on the East Coast.

As I got closer and our eyes met, I saw that hers were deep blue like the ocean.

The brief ceremony became a blur. I hadn't been able to keep my eyes off Aine.

"Hi," I said, intercepting her as she walked between clusters of people.

She put her hand on her heart.

"I didn't mean to startle you," I said, holding out my hand. "I'm Striker."

"I'm Aine." She put her hand in mine. "It's nice to meet you...uh...Striker."

"Actually, it's Griffin. Griffin Ellis."

"Right," she said, motioning toward Razor, Gunner, and some of the other guys. "You all have special names."

"I'm not sure there's anything special about them."

"I like Griffin."

"Thanks. I like Aine."

She smiled, her cheeks flushed, and she looked at her hand still clasped in mine, but she didn't pull away.

"Do you know if there will be dancing later?" God, had I really just asked her that? There had to be fewer than thirty people standing on the sand, most barefooted. I wondered if they'd even have food.

"Actually, there will be."

"Food?"

"No." She laughed. "Dancing. Are you hungry?"

"Maybe a little. I can go grab something—"

"Come with me," she said, pulling me by the hand that was still holding hers.

"Where are we going?"

"Kitchen. It's this place where they have...*food*."

Damn, she was even prettier when she smiled.

"What?" she asked when I didn't move but didn't let go of her hand either.

"You're beautiful," I murmured, getting closer to her.

"Thanks. You're not so bad yourself."

***

After that, we'd talked almost every day. The only time we didn't was when I was on a mission, and even then, I tried to schedule video calls with her as often as I could.

Aine was funny and smart, and she took my breath away when she smiled and when she lay naked in my bed.

There were days when we spent the entire day there, pleasuring one another's bodies. She'd once asked if her lack of sexual experience disappointed me, and I'd assured her it didn't—I loved that I was the one to take her from tentative to aggressive. I taught her the way to bring me pleasure and brought her to heights she said she'd never known were possible.

I loved sinking into her curvy softness. When she felt self-conscious, I convinced her that there wasn't a woman on earth I found as sexy and sensual as she was.

And then, I'd turned around and broken her spirit. I'd pushed her away with an excuse that made her doubt herself and sink deeper into insecurity. I hated that I'd done that to her, but I hadn't had a choice. What I'd learned after my sister's death would hurt her far more than the demise of our relationship had.

I only hoped the plumber saw the same exquisite beauty—inside and out—that I did. I prayed he'd encourage her to find her dreams and follow them, and help her know that no matter what had happened in her past, she could overcome the hurt and fear.

I walked over to the kitchen window and watched as she hugged her friend again and again, crying tears of happiness while a smile lit up her face. It warmed my heart. I turned around; Razor was studying me.

"A blind man could see how much you love my sister-in-law."

"She's better off without me."

"Good thing you gave her the choice," Razor added, leaving me standing alone in the kitchen while he went out to greet Mercer and his wife.

As I told Razor before, if I had, she would've told me it didn't matter. She would've told me that she'd stick by me no matter what, even if it meant we couldn't have the family we'd so often talked about.

The first time Aine had asked if I wanted to have children, I told her I didn't think I'd make a very good father. My lack of having my own in my life had made me wonder if I would know how to love a child in the way a father should.

She said she worried about the same thing. Her mother was a recovering alcoholic who hadn't spent much time with her or her sister when they were growing up. They spent their youth at boarding school and rarely saw their mother or father, even for holidays.

I remembered that the more she spoke, the more I knew she'd make a fantastic mother. So often, her personality, the way she treated people, even the way she smiled, reminded me of Aunt Dorothy. That she'd never had children was a tragedy I couldn't impose on Aine. Any child would be fortunate to have her as a mother.

"You remember Mercer," said Razor, coming back into the kitchen with our friend and colleague.

"Of course I do." I shook his hand.

"I haven't been gone that long, Raze," said the man those in the intelligence world knew as Eighty-eight.

"Feels that way. More so for those three though," Razor added, pointing at Aine, Ava, and Quinn. "Lots of luck getting your wife's attention now, man."

Mercer smiled. "I've had her undivided attention for months. I can share."

I, on the other hand, hadn't had Aine's attention, and I found myself craving it, no matter how much I knew I shouldn't.

When I looked over to where the three women sat in the living room, she turned her head and our eyes met. The smile she gave me settled over me like the warmest blanket. I wished so much I could accept the love she so freely gave me, but I couldn't. I loved her too much in return to do that to her.

14

Aine

"You look fantastic," I said to Quinn, hugging her for the tenth time.

"Thanks. I feel fantastic."

"Tell us about everywhere you've been. God, it feels like we haven't seen you in years," said Ava.

Quinn laughed. "On one hand, it feels as though we were just here yesterday, and on the other hand, I agree with you. How are Penelope and Tara?"

"They're planning to be here for Thanksgiving."

Quinn clapped her hands. "The tribe will be back together again. We haven't been since Ava and Razor's wedding. By the way, didn't you and Striker get together?"

"It was short-lived."

"Really?" asked Quinn, looking over at Striker. "He can't take his eyes off you."

"We'll tell you more about that later, when we're alone," said Ava.

Quinn looked back and forth between me and my sister. "I'm intrigued."

"Maybe you can help us solve the mystery."

Quinn stood. "I could use a walk on the beach. What about you two?"

Ava laughed. "I have to finish getting dinner ready, but we'll have our chance soon enough. My guess is that when we're finished eating, the K19 boys will retreat downstairs and hole themselves up in my husband's office."

"Mercer has a lot of catching up to do," agreed Quinn.

"Come keep me company in the kitchen."

Quinn and I followed Ava and stepped aside when she shooed the three men out of our way. As he passed, Striker's arm brushed mine. I felt it from the top of my head to my toes, and judging by the look on his face, he felt it too.

I couldn't wait to get Quinn's take on Striker's sudden shift in our relationship. Maybe she could help me figure why his sister's death had played such an integral role in our breakup.

"I had no idea what a good cook you were," said Quinn, eyeing the four courses Ava was busy putting the finishing touches on.

"I love it. How could you not in a kitchen like this?" Ava waved her arm around the large space. "The one in our house in Yachats is even better."

"I remember," said Quinn, dipping a spoon into the sauce Ava was preparing. "Oh my God, that's so good."

"Steak Diane is one of Tabon's favorites."

At the same time she mentioned his name, Tabon walked into the kitchen with a platter of rib eyes. "The ones on the right are medium rare, and those on the left are closer to well done. Let them rest for a few minutes."

"Yes, sir," she teased.

Tabon put his arms around Ava's waist. "I'll open another bottle of wine."

"Oh my goodness," gasped Ava. "I didn't even offer Quinn anything to drink."

"That's okay. I haven't forgotten how to ask."

"Would you like a glass?" Tabon asked as he pulled the cork.

"No, thanks. I'll stick with water."

Both Ava and I spun around at the same time, and when we did, Quinn nodded her head and patted her belly.

"Four months."

We squealed and fell into a group hug.

"I'm so happy for you."

"To be honest, I was a little worried about how you'd feel—you know, being around the baby," said Ava.

"Where is Sam anyway?"

"Still napping," I answered, pointing to the baby monitor sitting on the kitchen counter. "I guarantee he'll wake up as soon as we sit down for dinner."

Sure enough, the minute the serving dishes were on the table and Ava had taken a seat, we heard Sam's wails through the monitor.

"I'll get him," I offered.

"Thanks, sis."

I was almost to the baby's room when I met Striker coming out of the restroom.

"Where are you off to?"

"To get Sam." I pointed to the door. "Although by the sound of it, he may have fallen back to sleep."

I peeked my head in and saw the baby's eyes were open. "There he is," I said, plucking him out of the crib. "Do you need a diaper change, sweet boy?"

When I carried him over to the changing table, I noticed that Striker still stood in the doorway.

"Do you want to help?"

He held up both of his hands. "I can assure you that I won't be any help whatsoever. In fact, I'll probably make it harder on both of you."

"Changing a baby isn't as complicated as extracting kidnapping victims from a foreign country, Striker." By the time I finished my sentence, though, I was done putting on a new diaper and changing the baby's clothes.

"You're really good at that."

"I've had a lot of practice."

"Your sister is lucky to have you around."

"I'm the lucky one," I said, nuzzling Sam. "I love him so much."

I watched as Striker's smile turned into a frown, no matter how hard he tried to mask it. It was another clue. Seeing me holding my nephew made him happy and sad at the same time. What was that all about?

"We should get back. They might be waiting for us to start eating."

"Right," he said, motioning for me to go by him. For the second time today, our bodies brushed against each other. This time, I heard his quick intake of breath. If he was so affected by our touch, why in God's name had he broken up with me? I felt as though the question had burned itself on my brain, and most of the time, it was all I could think about.

I stopped and looked into his eyes. I was close enough that, if I wanted to, I could bring my lips to his. Instead, I held my breath as he stroked his finger down the baby's cheek and then mine. The sadness in his eyes as he did almost brought me to tears.

15

Striker

I should ask Razor if tomorrow we could work anywhere but here, where I'd likely run into Aine multiple times a day. I knew my teammate would refuse, and I couldn't blame him. Why be away from his gorgeous wife and son when he didn't have to be?

"Where are you staying?" Mercer asked as we were getting ready to leave.

"The house in Harmony."

"Spent many nights there," Mercer commented. "I have to admit, I don't miss it."

"How's your new place coming along?" Razor asked.

"It's inhabitable," Quinn answered, laughing. "That's all I can say about it."

Mercer pulled her closer to him and kissed her forehead. "We'll get there, precious."

"We better hurry," she said, rubbing her belly. "We have to finish the nursery at least."

"Congratulations again," said Razor, shaking Mercer's hand.

"Same," I said, holding my hand out too, somewhat surprised at my own sincerity. I didn't remember ever caring one way or another when someone said they were having a baby, or had had one.

"Thanks," said Mercer. "I know Quinn said we have to have the nursery done, but I'm determined to have the whole house finished before our baby is born."

"When's that?" I asked, surprising myself a second time. Since when did I pay attention to shit like this?

"Late April if the doctor's got it right."

I watched Aine and Ava both hug Quinn as though it was the last time they'd see her for a while.

"See you tomorrow?" she said to both of them, making me smile.

"We have to start planning your baby shower," said Ava.

When I looked at Aine, she was looking at me.

"Walk me out?" I asked.

"Uh...sure."

I thanked Razor and Ava, told them I'd be back the next day, and put my hand on the small of Aine's back as we walked out the door.

"I had a nice time tonight," I said, trying to sound more like her friend than her lover, but having a hard time not falling into the rhythms of when we used to be a couple.

"I did too. It was so good to see Quinn again."

"I'll be back tomorrow."

"I heard."

"Will you be okay with me being around so much?"

She shrugged. "I might not be."

I looked into her eyes. "Still leaving?"

"No. I'm sorry. That wasn't nice."

"I get it, but I meant what I said before, Aine. I want us to be friends."

"Are you friends with all your previous lovers?"

I had to think about it for a minute, but yeah, I was with the ones I still saw occasionally, like Merrigan.

"Good night, Striker," she said before I could answer or give in to the temptation to kiss her goodnight.

The drive from Razor's duplex to Harmony was short, but like Mercer said about the place, it wasn't a house I'd miss staying in if there was another option. Maybe tomorrow I'd see if I could find something closer to the beach, so I'd be able to enjoy my time here a little more.

When Aine said she liked to listen to the ocean before she went to sleep, I'd envied her. Maybe I could rent a place where I could open up the sliding doors, or even windows, and listen to the waves crashing all night long. I doubted if they would actually lull me to sleep, and if they did, I wouldn't stay that way for very long.

In my line of work, sleep was a luxury, whether it was because I was on a mission or because I was reliving a past one.

"What the hell am I doing?" I turned the car around and drove back to Moonstone Beach. I drove up to Cambria Shores Inn and breathed a sigh of relief when I saw the vacancy sign lit up. There was no reason for me to stay in a shit-hole safe house until I found a place to rent. Instead, I'd stay here, the place where Aine and I had stayed the first time we had sex.

"Griffin Ellis," I told the woman behind the desk when she asked my name.

"Mr. Ellis, welcome back. It's so good to see you again."

I couldn't say that I remembered seeing her before, but I had had quite a lot on my mind the last time I was here.

"You're in luck. Room four is available if you'd like it."

"Sure. Thanks," I responded, not knowing whether it was a good idea to relive every detail of being here with Aine.

Once I had the key, I moved my car to the parking spot in front of the room and carried my bag inside. The old motor lodge had been refurbished a couple of years ago with new furniture and bathrooms. I wasn't sure if the fireplace had been there all along and they'd refaced it, or if it had been added. Either way, it was a nice touch.

The best part, though, was that I could step outside the door and feel the mist from the ocean on my face. With the window open, I could hear the same waves crashing that I imagined Aine was hearing.

I closed my eyes and pictured her lying on the bed, the windows open even though it was chilly, or even sitting out on the deck of the house, like she had in Yachats.

Pulling back the comforter, I couldn't help but remember the last time I'd been in this same room, only then I'd been with Aine.

***

The look of vulnerability on Aine's face had the opposite effect of the one it should have had on me. My need only accelerated when I thought about how nervous she was. I stood in front of her, taking the pins out of her hair and dropping them on the table next to us.

"I've thought about weaving my fingers in your hair so many times," I said, stroking gently at first, knowing soon I wouldn't be able to be.

I scooped her in my arms with a sudden movement and took two steps to the bed, setting her down on it.

"You have the most beautiful skin," I said as I stroked the soft spot beneath her ear. "Has anyone told you how soft it is?"

"No one. Only you."

"Has anyone kissed you here, Aine? You can tell me the truth."

I trailed my lips from her ear, back to her neck, holding her hair out of my way so I could run my tongue down her spine. Aine's fingers gripped the bedding, and chill bumps covered her exposed skin. If this was her reaction to simple kisses, I couldn't imagine how responsive she'd be once I got her naked.

"The things I want to do to you," I murmured.

"I want you to. Everything you want, I want you to do it."

My fingers slid between the fabric of her blouse and her skin until I felt the clasp of her bra. I unfastened it—wanting everything at once. I wished I could magically remove her shirt and pants at the same time so she'd instantly be naked before me. Instead, I stood. If it couldn't be quick, I'd savor it.

"Stand and remove your clothes, Aine." The same look of vulnerability I'd seen moments ago settled on her face. "Do it, Aine. Let me see you. I want to see all of you."

Her fingers visibly trembled as she did as I asked, removing every piece of clothing covering the most perfect body I'd ever seen.

Her breasts were plump and heavy, with rose-colored nipples that pulled tight into nubs hardened by her desire.

"Come closer to me," I said, sitting in the chair and opening my legs so she could stand before me, close enough to touch.

I started at her face, running my fingers over her lips, down her chin, to her neck. I flattened both hands and grasped each of her breasts at the same time. She gasped when I kneaded them, likely harder than anyone ever had before.

I could only be gentle so long, and it was best she learned that upfront. I'd take possession of her body without hesitation, and if she didn't like it, I would know we didn't belong together. Something told me that she wouldn't disappoint. My hands trailed farther down her body, pulling her closer so I could feel every inch of her, own every inch of her.

"Do I scare you?" I asked.

"Not at all."

"Don't lie to me, Aine." I put my hands on her waist and held tight.

"Touch me," she pleaded, arching her back to bring her sex closer to me.

Unable to resist her pleas, I forced her back on the bed. Her eyes widened as she watched me shed my clothes.

"Spread your legs, Aine. I want to look at you."

She didn't hesitate.

"Touch yourself, baby. Show me how much you want me."

Her fingers trailed to the place between her legs where I couldn't wait to have my own hands and mouth.

"Eyes open," I said, lowering myself over her and taking one nipple between my teeth. "Did I tell you to stop touching yourself?" I asked between nips of her flesh.

"No," she stammered.

I took my time making my way down her body until my mouth was where her fingers were. I grasped her wrist and brought them to my mouth. She groaned when I licked away her wetness.

"Still, Aine," I said when her body began to writhe.

"I can't," she moaned. "God, Griffin, I need you."

"Soon, baby," I soothed, putting my mouth back on her.

By the time I was ready to join our bodies together, Aine was almost in tears.

"I can't," she said each time I coaxed her to the plateau of another orgasm.

"You can. Do it for me, Aine. Show me how good I make you feel."

When I brought my body to hers and entered her for the first time, I came close to climaxing the minute I was inside her.

"Be still," I said as I had before.

She calmed herself, taking deep breaths.

"Look at me."

She opened her glistening eyes, keeping their focus on mine.

"It's perfect," I moaned. "You're perfect."

I couldn't quell the urgency I felt now that I was finally with the woman I'd spent so many nights dreaming of.

* * *

Sex between us had only gotten better. If I'd been asked to define the perfect woman, it would be Aine. Whenever we were together, it was impossible for me to keep my hands off her.

When we'd touched by accident today, I felt the same sense of urgency to take her and make her mine that I had every other time our skin had come in contact.

There had been no woman before, and there'd be no woman after who would be as perfect as she was.

That I couldn't have her, couldn't claim her as mine forever, tore me up inside. Sure, I could be a selfish bastard and tell her the real reason I'd broken up with her. I could accept it when she told me it didn't matter. She might even suggest we adopt children, just so she could be with me.

None of that would change the fact that the same thing may live inside of me as had my sister. Whether it manifested itself now or never, I couldn't risk putting Aine through it. She'd already been through too much.

Her father had been a monster. I couldn't be the man who forced her to live her life with me when I knew I could be just as monstrous. I was damaged, and there was nothing either of us could do about it.

I didn't remember crying before my aunt died, or since, but tonight I let the tears flow freely. I felt the loss of Aine as profoundly now as I had the day she'd walked out of my condo and out of my life, not because she'd wanted to, but because I'd forced her to.

16

Aine

"What are you thinking about?" asked Ava, coming out onto the deck where I stood listening to the sounds of the ocean.

"The same thing I'm always thinking about."

"You could always ask Tabon."

"Ask him what? Why my boyfriend broke up with me? You've got to be kidding."

"I could ask him."

"I'll tell you what I was really thinking about, Ava. I was standing out here, wondering if I could possibly make a bigger fool of myself tomorrow than I did today. I'm like Dasher—a little puppy who follows Striker around, hoping he'll pay attention to me."

"You weren't following him around. He came to you."

"Because he had to. He had to check on me, make sure I was okay. God, I make myself sick. I can't imagine how he must be feeling."

"Is this one of those times that whatever I have to say is unsolicited?"

"Go ahead, tell me what you think, but be gentle."

"He can't stay away from you. Every time he went to you today, it was his own choice. No one asked him to."

"He heard you and Tabon talking about me."

"So? He doesn't seem like the kind of man who would stick his nose into anything he didn't want to."

My phone vibrated, and I plucked it from my back pocket. "It's Stuart. I should take it."

When Ava nodded and went inside, I accepted the call.

"Hi," I said, taking a deep breath and trying to erase the image I had of Striker in my head and replace it with Stuart's likeness instead.

"I know you just left, but I miss you."

"You're right. It's only been a day."

"I guess that means you don't miss me."

"That isn't what I said."

"Have you figured out how long you'll be there?"

"Not yet. Like I said, I just got here."

"What about Thanksgiving?"

I'd invited Penelope and Tara for the holiday without considering that Stuart might want to spend it with me. Would it be too awkward if I invited him too?

"Radio silence."

"I'm sorry. I was just thinking about whether you'd want to come here."

"Is that an invitation?"

"Y-yes."

"You sure about that?"

I cleared my throat. What was wrong with me? "Yes, Stuart. It's an invitation. Would you please come to Cambria for Thanksgiving?"

"I'd love to. Although, I have to admit, I was hoping you'd invite me down before that."

"Really? Don't you have to work?"

"I can get one of the guys to cover me next weekend, unless you have other plans."

I half laughed. "What other plans would I have?"

"I don't know, maybe with that guy that works with your brother-in-law, who can't seem to keep his eyes off you."

"You're imagining things."

"Right."

I heard him sigh.

"I can't wait to see you, Aine."

"Um, I can text you the address if you want." I rolled my eyes. How else would he find me? "Do you want some suggestions of places to stay?"

"I guess that means I won't be staying with you."

"What? I mean, you can, but you never…"

"Maybe it's time I did."

I couldn't believe Friday, and Stuart's visit, was only three days away. How had the last week passed so quickly? Ava, Sam, and I had spent each day with Quinn since Mercer was at the house too, working with Razor, Monk, and Striker.

Between how busy we'd been and the fact that Striker always seemed to be at the house, I hadn't had time to talk to Tabon about him.

Every afternoon, I'd gone for a run with Dasher, and when I returned, Striker would sometimes be waiting for me in the grassy area near the deck.

"I could go with you this weekend," he said today when I met him at the top of the trail.

"Um…I'm taking a break."

"Rest day?"

"Something like that."

"Why do I feel as though you aren't telling me the whole story?"

I sat down on the grass and rubbed Dasher's tummy. "Stuart is visiting this weekend."

Striker sat down next to me. "I see, and you're uncomfortable talking about it."

"I know I shouldn't be. I mean, we're just friends, right?"

"It doesn't mean it won't be awkward the first few times we see each other with someone else."

I felt sick to my stomach. I couldn't handle seeing Striker with another woman. Not now and maybe never.

"Are you seeing someone else?" I asked, not wanting to hear the answer but knowing I had to force myself to find out.

"No," he said, shaking his head. "It's far more likely that you'll be married and have a family before I find time to date again."

I brought my knees closer to my body and wrapped my arms around them.

"This is a conversation I'd rather not have," I admitted.

"It isn't easy for me either, Aine."

Inside, I was screaming, *then why did you break up with me?* But outside, I looked at the ocean. "Would it be easier if I wasn't here?" I asked.

Striker shook his head. "I don't want you to leave on my account."

"So, you're fine with Stuart visiting?"

"Everything will be okay, Aine. Do whatever you want to do. Don't take me into account."

"I can't tell if you're being sarcastic or sincere."

Striker stood and brushed the sandy grass from his pants. "I let you go, Aine. I have no right to ask that you do anything but live your life."

Thankfully, he went inside before I could respond. If he hadn't, I would've told him that he didn't have to ask. If he said he wanted me to, I'd run back into his arms and wouldn't give Stuart another thought.

But that wasn't what Striker wanted. As he said, he let me go. He didn't say he wanted me back.

17

Striker

"I heard back from the Bogotá consulate. Your meeting with the Cuban is set."

"When?" I asked Razor.

"As soon as you can make arrangements to leave."

If there were ever an indication of fate intervening in my life, it was now. Instead of having to spend the weekend holed up in my room on Moonstone Beach in order to avoid seeing Aine with the plumber, I'd be on a mission in South America.

"Where's Onyx?"

"On standby."

I called the K19 pilot, and we agreed to meet at the airfield at eighteen hundred hours.

"The Harmony house is on your way, but go ahead if you need to leave now," Razor said when I told him the plan we'd made.

"I'm not staying there. I got a room on Moonstone Beach." I'd planned to see if I could rent a house, but I'd settled into the inn and decided not to move.

Razor nodded. "Like I said, do what you have to do."

My first inclination was to find Aine and tell her I was leaving, but should I? Would she wonder why I sought her out when, per my request, we were nothing more than friends? Or would she be hurt and angry if I left without saying goodbye?

"Got a minute?" asked Mercer, laying out several documents on the table in front of us.

"What have you pieced together?"

Mercer had been working on the forensic accounting for the last few days, some of which were productive, and some of which were frustrating. I hoped he had something worthwhile to share with me.

"The Islamics in Buenaventura have done a good job covering their tracks to this point. There is no history of money transfers. However, today I found out why."

Mercer pointed to several of the transactions on the printouts. "Without monitoring the activity every day, we would've missed these. The transactions are purged at the close of business."

I mentally added the totals; the final figure was in the millions, and that was only for one day. "Jesus," I muttered. "There's no end to what Ghafor could do with this kind of money."

"We have to stop him," said Mercer, looking me in the eye. "I don't think we can afford to wait any longer."

Until now, I'd believed Ghafor was limping along in the same way he had for the last two years. That was no longer the case. There was too much money, which translated into weapons and payoffs. "I agree."

"Do we act before or after Bogotá?" asked Razor.

"After. It's likely the last chance we'll have to find out who's running the show in Buenaventura."

"Copy that," said Razor, going back to the monitors.

"Any leads yet?" I asked Mercer.

"Not yet, but catching the money was the first step. Now that I have, I can start tracing it."

Something nagged at me. It couldn't be as simple as the Colombian fundamentalists supplying the Islamic State leader with that kind of money. They'd never be able to raise as much cash as had been transferred today, not to mention how many other days similar amounts had been moved.

More likely, the money was coming from someone with much deeper pockets. There were two possibilities. First, one of the drug cartels was supplying the money. Second, any country that considered the United States an enemy, and there were too many of those to count. It could be anywhere from Venezuela to Russia.

"Who's going with you to Bogotá?" Mercer asked.

"Ranger and Diesel, along with Onyx and Corazón."

"Get in and out as quickly as you can," said Mercer.

"I hear you."

"Godspeed," said Razor as I walked out of the office and up the stairs.

I made a decision as I took each step. If I ran into Aine, I'd tell her, but I wouldn't go looking for her.

I breathed a sigh of relief when I saw her sitting on the deck with her sister and Quinn. When I reached the top of the stairs and she looked straight at me, I motioned for her to come inside.

"What's up?" she asked, eyeing my laptop bag. "Quitting early today?"

"Actually, I have to leave town."

"Oh." She put her hands in her pockets.

"I shouldn't be gone more than a week."

"If you're leaving because of Stuart..."

"I promise I'm not." Although I wasn't complaining about having an excuse not to be here.

"Okay. Well, stay safe."

I leaned forward, as though Aine's lips had a magnetic pull. If she hadn't turned her head at the last possible moment, I would've kissed her mouth rather than her cheek.

"I'm sorry," I mumbled. "Habit, I guess. I didn't mean—"

"Goodbye, Striker." She walked away, but I still saw her reddened cheeks.

"Aine, wait."

She turned but didn't walk back over to me.

"I'm sorry," I said a second time.

"Me too."

I swore all the way back to Moonstone Beach, got out of my car, went into my room, and swore some more. What the hell had I just done? It was as though I'd temporarily lost my mind.

Jesus, I'd almost kissed Aine like it was the most natural thing in the world. What upset me more than my dickhead move, was the way it left me feeling. If I could, I'd drive back to that house and ravage not only her lips, but every inch of her body.

Sex with Aine was always spectacular, but right before and right after a mission, it was especially so. I'd wring every ounce of pleasure from her body as though it would fortify me no matter what danger I faced. When I came home, I'd do the same thing, to fill the emptiness I'd felt every minute I was away from her.

We'd only been together a couple of months, but the relationship I'd had with Aine was so different than any I'd had prior, which made it feel like so much longer.

Being around her again after so many months of denying myself contact, brought everything we'd shared back to the surface. I could feel, smell, and even taste Aine, just by being near her. I was starved for her, and only her.

She'd asked if I was with someone else. No, I wasn't, and it wasn't likely I ever would be. Here I was, not quite forty, and facing celibacy for the rest of my life.

I'd apologized twice, but it still didn't feel like it was enough. It wasn't just the attempted kiss I needed to apologize for. I'd given her so many mixed signals, and that was unconscionably unfair.

The only solution I could come up with was to return to the East Coast and continue the mission from there. If I returned to Cambria, every time I saw Aine, I'd risk doing the same thing I'd done earlier.

18

Aine

Ava's eyes were open wide when I came back out on the deck. "What was that?"

"Habit."

"Huh?"

"That's what he said. First, he apologized, and then he said it was habit."

Ava looked at Quinn, who shook her head and held up her hands. "No comment."

"What a jerk."

I knew I should agree, say a few choice words against him, but the truth was, I was kicking myself for turning my head. If I hadn't, I would've had the chance to feel his lips on mine one more time.

"Are you okay?" Quinn asked, putting her arm around me.

I shook my head, and my eyes filled with tears. "I'm not."

"Oh, honey. I'm sorry." Ava stood and put her arm around me too.

"What can I do to help?" asked Quinn.

"Did you tell her about Striker's sister?"

I shook my head.

"Have a seat, girlfriend," Ava said to Quinn and then pulled out a chair for me. "I have to go get Sam, but you two can start without me."

"What's she talking about?" Quinn asked, leaning forward to wipe away my tears.

"I'm sure it's nothing."

"Tell me anyway."

Quinn didn't say much while I told her about Striker ending things right after he found out his sister died. However, I knew Quinn well enough that I could tell she was formulating a plan.

"Remember when I first started seeing Mercer?"

I nodded.

"I had some questions about him, and you suggested we look him up on the internet."

"Yeah?"

"Have you considered researching his sister's death?"

"No."

"It's worth a shot, right?"

"I don't know what that would achieve."

"Maybe you'll find something that will give you a clue as to why it affected Striker the way it did. I mean, it's kind of your specialty, Aine."

Quinn was right, it was. However, the research I'd conducted to get my degree was based in science, not hypothesis. The brain's physical reaction had been my focus, not a theoretical emotional response. It would take at least a master's degree if not a doctorate for me to take my research to the behavioral analysis level.

Still, knowing something about Striker's sister's death may give me some idea why it had shaken him so much that he'd reevaluated our relationship enough to end it.

"There's nothing," I said to Quinn and Ava after I'd spent an hour surfing the net.

"What are you looking for?" Tabon asked, coming into the kitchen.

I waited for Ava to answer him. "What the hell?" I mouthed when she didn't.

"We're researching something."

Tabon raised a brow. "What are you up to, Avarie?"

My sister made a growling sound. "It really isn't any of your business, but Aine is trying to find out what happened to Striker's sister."

"Oh."

The three of us turned and looked at him.

"You know something, don't you?" Ava asked her husband.

Tabon scrubbed his face with his hand. "I'm going to kill Striker, unless he kills me first." He pulled out a chair and sat down next to me. I studied his face. Whatever Tabon was about to say would be breaking a confidence, and that wasn't fair to him or to Striker.

"Don't tell me," I said.

"What?" gasped Ava.

"I'm serious," I said, looking between my sister and brother-in-law. "If Striker asked you not to tell me, then you shouldn't."

"I disagree," said Ava, folding her arms. "If Striker wasn't honest with my sister, then you need to tell her the truth."

"Come with me."

When Tabon stood and held his hand out, I was tempted to refuse to go with him. Whatever he was about to tell me was something he didn't want to say in front of Ava or Quinn.

"What do you know about Striker's family?" he asked once we were out on the deck and he'd closed the sliding glass door behind us.

"Just that his parents are both dead, as is his aunt, who raised him."

"Did he tell you much about his mother and father?"

"A little. I know neither of them were in his life."

"Both of his parents were addicts—drugs and alcohol."

"I figured it was something like that."

"His sister was too."

"Okay."

"Striker may have some concern about genetic predisposition."

"Based on what?"

"You're aware that addictive personalities can be, at least in part, genetic. A lot of things that may have once been considered strictly behavioral, we're finding may be more nature than nurture."

I nodded. "My degree is in neuroscience, Tabon."

"I know it is. So, whether Striker is willing to admit it or not, you can understand where he's coming from."

I thought over what Tabon had just said. Could that be what was behind our breakup? It didn't make sense. He'd known about his family members' addictions long before we'd started seeing each other. To say his sister's death was the impetus that made him realize he was "predisposed" didn't make sense. There had to be more to it.

"There's something you're not telling me."

Tabon shook his head. "I can't, Aine. It's Striker's story, not mine. I know your sister will disagree with me. She may even insist I tell you everything I know, but before we came out here, you told me not to tell you anything. Instead, I've told you as much as you could've figured out on your own."

I put my hand on Tabon's arm. "I meant what I said. I wouldn't ask you to betray a confidence."

"And I won't ask you to lie to your sister."

"I won't. I'll tell her what you told me, not what you didn't."

Tabon nodded. "Thanks."

"We haven't had a chance to talk about what Tabon told you," said Ava a couple of days later, while looking over her shoulder as she watched her husband and Mercer go down the stairs to the office.

"It wasn't that interesting."

"Well, what was it?" Ava pushed.

I sighed and looked between my sister and Quinn. "Striker's sister was a drug addict. Although he didn't say she died of an overdose, her death had something to do with her addiction."

"Is he embarrassed?" Ava asked.

"I don't think someone like Striker would be embarrassed about that, Ava," Quinn answered for me.

"Both of his parents were addicts too."

Ava looked lost, but Quinn looked thoughtful.

"Evidently, he's concerned about genetic predisposition."

"Makes sense, but didn't he know his parents were addicts long before you and he started seeing each other?"

"That's exactly what I said, Quinn."

"Huh."

"I know."

"There has to be more to it," Ava chimed in. "Tabon didn't know anything more?"

"Again, I said essentially the same thing."

"But he didn't tell you anything else?"

"That's right."

"If he suddenly became concerned about hereditary issues, he must've found something out about his sister that he wasn't aware of when they were growing up."

I looked at Quinn. That made perfect sense. "But what?"

"That's the unanswered question."

"Is there any way for either of our husbands to find out more?" asked Ava.

"I'm not sure," answered Quinn, "but the best person I can think of to talk to about it, isn't either one of them."

"Who?" I asked, hoping she wouldn't say Striker.

"Merrigan."

I looked at my watch. "I need to leave."

"That's right, the new beau is coming to visit. I can't wait to meet him," said Quinn, rubbing her hands together.

Ava smiled, but it didn't reach her eyes. "He's a really nice guy."

I inwardly groaned. Was that the best she could come up with?

"What's wrong?" asked Quinn.

"Nothing. Frustrated. Trying to understand. But why? I'm with Stuart now."

"Sweetie..."

"I know. It's stupid."

"I didn't say that."

I looked into Quinn's eyes. "What should I do?"

"You know what to do. Follow your heart."

I nodded. "I gotta go."

Quinn winked. "Go on then, get outta here, girl."

19

Striker

We hadn't been on the ground an hour and were headed to the US embassy in Bogotá when I received a call from the ambassador.

"Juan Carlos is dead."

"*Goddammit*," I swore under my breath. "Sorry, sir." I knew better than to use that kind of language with a high-ranking US diplomat.

"I understand and share your frustration. Details regarding your visit were kept on a need-to-know basis."

"Which means either you have a mole or we do."

"It's more likely on our end."

"Yes, sir," I responded, relieved the ambassador said it, so I didn't have to.

"I'm afraid you've made a wasted trip."

"I realize you may not have time in your schedule to meet with us, but I'm asking anyway, sir."

"Least I could do. What's your ETA?"

"Less than five minutes."

"I'll be waiting."

I ended the call and told Ranger and Diesel what the ambassador and I had discussed.

"I'll see what I can find out while you're in the meeting," offered Diesel.

"Ranger, you join me."

"Roger that," he answered.

Once we arrived, I'd request our meeting be private. It would be up to Diesel to figure out who wouldn't want it to be.

I wished Onyx and Corazón had come with us rather than stayed with the plane. I could've used two more sets of eyes to be on the lookout for the mole.

20

Aine

"I sense you have some discomfort over me staying with you," Stuart said on the ride back from the airport.

I bit my lower lip. "The change in your attitude was just so...unexpected."

"I'm sorry, Aine. I was...reacting."

I kept both hands firmly on the steering wheel and didn't look at him. "To what?"

"The guy, the one you said works with your sister's husband."

"He does work with Tabon."

"It's obvious that he's interested in you, Aine."

I took a deep breath and let it out slowly. "We dated, briefly. It ended a long time ago."

Out of the corner of my eye, I saw Stuart nod.

"I figured it was something like that."

"I'm sorry I didn't tell you before, but honestly, it's old news."

"Is it?"

"It is, Stuart."

We were almost to the turnoff for Cambria before Stuart spoke again.

"I booked a place to stay."

"Uh, okay. Where?"

"Someplace called Cambria Shores."

I knew my cheeks were flaming red, but there was little I could do about it.

"Are you okay?"

"I'm fine, just a little warm." I fiddled with the air conditioner and turned the vents so they were pointed directly at me. "Do you want to come by the house first?"

"Either way. I guess we could stop so I can check in."

"Sure."

Instead of going left at the turnoff to the house, I turned right to go to Moonstone Beach. I pulled into the inn's parking lot and went inside with Stuart.

"You look so familiar," said the woman behind the desk.

"I get that a lot. I'm a twin."

"I see," said the woman, looking puzzled. "What is your name again?"

"Aine," I answered.

"I remember you. You were here last year with—"

"My mom. She isn't here this year, so I'm staying with my sister and her husband who have a home on Windsor."

Stuart had finished filling out the paperwork and was staring at me. "Are you sure you're okay?"

"Yep," I answered, doing my best not to roll my eyes. "Fine and dandy." It could've been worse. At least the woman hadn't mentioned Griffin.

"Oh, Mr. Ellis, you're back sooner than you expected!" exclaimed the woman, looking beyond Stuart and me.

It couldn't be. Could it? I turned around and came face-to-face with Striker.

"What are you doing here?" I asked.

"I could ask you the same thing."

"Oh, um, Stuart is just checking in."

Striker studied me but didn't say another word.

"Ready?" I asked, seeing that Stuart had the room key in his hand. "Do you want to drop your bags off or do that later?"

"Now's good."

I almost offered to wait in the car, but if Stuart had something to say, now would be as good a time as any for me to listen.

"That was awkward," he said after the office door closed behind us.

"He was supposed to be in South America." I sighed and then immediately wondered if I should've divulged that information. Would Stuart think I only invited him to visit because Striker should have been out of the country?

"It would've been less awkward if you'd introduced us."

"Oh, God, I'm sorry. I forgot you hadn't met before."

"You seem flustered," Stuart commented.

"What? No. Like I said before, I'm fine."

"Are you sure you want me here?"

"Yes, Stuart. I want you here." I folded my arms. "As I told you, Striker and I were together a while ago, and now we're not. It's not something I'm going to continue to apologize for."

He held up both of his hands. "No apology necessary. I was merely wondering if there was unfinished business between the two of you."

"There isn't."

I chose to ignore the doubtful expression on Stuart's face. "Ready?" I asked for the second time once he'd put his bag inside the room.

"Sure."

I watched Stuart, who was checking out the view from the deck.

"Doesn't look much different than Yachats. Why does your brother-in-law own houses in two such similar places?"

"You know, that's a good question. You should ask him."

Stuart nodded.

"I was going to get a glass of wine. Can I get you anything?"

"A beer would be nice if they have it."

"I'm sure they do. Be right back."

"Everything okay?" asked Ava, who was in the kitchen with Tabon and Sam.

"No. Nothing is okay."

"Anything I can do to help?" Tabon asked.

"Take Stuart a beer so I can have a couple of minutes to get my shit together."

"Not a problem." Tabon grabbed two bottles from the fridge and left me alone with my sister and the baby.

"What is going on?" Ava asked.

"Striker is back."

"Already?"

"That's what I said. Maybe I didn't say that exactly. I think I asked him what he was doing at the inn."

"Wait. What?"

"Stuart was checking into the inn on Moonstone Beach, and Striker walked into the office at the same time."

"I'm so confused." Ava buckled Sam into the high chair. "Why was Stuart checking into the inn?"

"We aren't...we haven't...you know."

"You're kidding."

I shook my head. "I don't think he believes in sex before marriage, or maybe it's just sex before two people love each other that he's against."

"Wow."

"It's fine, Ava."

"It's weird is what it is."

"I don't have a problem with it."

"That's a problem in and of itself."

I peered out to the deck. It looked like Stuart and Tabon were in the midst of a conversation. Thank God.

"Look, I don't want to talk about it right now. We can talk more later after I take Stuart back. Who's supposed to be here for dinner tonight?" I pulled out a chair and sat down. The stress from both Striker and Stuart being here—just being around Striker in general—was wreaking havoc on my stomach.

"You, Stuart, Tabon, and me, and maybe Quinn and Mercer." Ava pulled out the chair next to me. "Are you okay? You look kind of pale."

"I think I'm giving myself an ulcer." I rubbed my stomach.

Ava reached over and felt my forehead. "You might be getting sick. What are your symptoms?"

"My stomach hurts. Otherwise, I feel fine."

"How long has it hurt?"

"I don't know, Doctor Ava, maybe since Striker decided to show up."

Ava rolled her eyes. "You can't let this make you sick, Aine. Maybe you should try meditating."

"I meditate every time I go for a run."

"I don't think it's helping."

"Can we get back to what we were talking about before?"

"I don't remember what that was."

"I think I was about to say that maybe I'll get lucky and I won't run into Striker again before Stuart goes back to Yachats."

"Uh-oh," said Ava, standing and looking out the window.

"What? Don't tell me. He's here, isn't he?"

Ava nodded.

"Why?"

She shrugged. "I don't know. What are you going to do?"

"I can see if Stuart wants to go out for dinner tonight, you know, just the two of us."

"If that's your plan, you better get outside before my husband ruins it. You know how Tabon is. The more the merrier. He's probably already asked him how he likes his steak."

"You two eat an awful lot of steak."

"Tabon eats a lot of steak. I fill up on the side dishes."

"Why don't you just tell him you don't like to eat so much red meat?"

"Seriously, Aine?"

"Right."

"She goes for a run almost every day," I heard Tabon say to Stuart when I came outside. "You should go with her tomorrow."

"I'm not much of a runner." Stuart rubbed his leg. "Plumber's knee."

Tabon turned when I closed the sliding door behind me. "I was just telling Stuart that it's time for me to fire up the grill."

"Oh, I was thinking we could go out tonight."

"Friday night in Cambria? You're kidding, right?"

Since Stuart wasn't looking, I glared at Tabon.

"Sorry," he mouthed.

"Saturday night is a better date night anyway," said Stuart, turning around to look at me. "Come have a seat," he added, motioning to the chair next to him.

"Where's your wine?" he asked when I sat down.

"It's right here," said Striker, coming out the sliding door and setting a glass in front of me. "I'm Striker. We didn't get a formal introduction earlier." He held his hand out to Stuart.

"Stuart Anderson. Aine's boyfriend."

"Nice to meet you, Stu."

I was ready to wipe the damn smirk right off Striker's face. What was he trying to do, intentionally ruin my relationship with Stuart?

"Got a minute, Razor?" he asked.

"Sure thing. Excuse us."

I waited until the two men were inside before I spoke. "Are you sure you wouldn't rather go out tonight?"

"That wouldn't be very hospitable." Stuart rubbed his chin. "If you're worried about me and your ex, I can handle myself just fine, darlin'."

"It isn't you I'm worried about. I mean it is, but not because you can't handle yourself."

"Look, either you're with me, or you're not. Best you let me know sooner rather than later if you're not."

"I'm with you, Stuart."

"Let's not worry about Striper, then."

"It's Striker."

"I know."

21

Striker

I'd drawn out my conversation with the innkeeper long enough to see that the plumber had only carried one bag into his room, shut the door, and then left with Aine.

It was an interesting development. When I was in Yachats, the night I took a walk on the trail down to her house, the plumber hadn't been there then either. Now, instead of staying with Aine, he was staying at the inn. And it didn't appear Aine was staying there with him. So what was the deal between them?

I hadn't planned to come over to Razor and Ava's this afternoon, but with that development, I wasn't able to stay away.

"I didn't think we'd see you until Monday. I thought you and the crew were taking the weekend off. Where's everyone else?"

"They returned to the East Coast since there was nothing happening."

Razor nodded. "And you?"

"I need to brief you on my meeting with the ambassador."

"Right. That couldn't have waited."

"It couldn't."

"Uh-huh. What's your deal, Striker? Either you want to be with Aine or you don't. Don't mess this up for her."

"I can leave—"

"I've told you before, don't be like that. I just want to make sure you're here for the right reason. If you believe I need to be briefed tonight, then let's do it."

"Will Mercer be here later?"

"Affirmative. Would you rather wait?"

I nodded.

"Then, let's have a beer."

I followed Razor upstairs and into the kitchen. From where I stood, I could see the plumber take Aine's hand and bring it to his lips. It was an intimate moment I wished I hadn't witnessed.

22

Aine

I sat on the same side of the table as Ava, leaving one seat in between and putting the farthest distance between Stuart and Striker I could manage. It wasn't difficult since Mercer had called to say Quinn wasn't feeling well and they wouldn't be able to make it to dinner.

Fortunately, Tabon kept Striker engaged throughout the meal. Although, every time I looked, my ex-boyfriend was looking at me.

Once Stuart went back to Yachats, I intended to have it out with him. I'd had enough of his seesaw behavior.

"Thanksgiving is less than a week away," Tabon said to Stuart. "You stickin' around for it?"

"That's up to Aine," he answered, looking at me.

"I'd love it if you would, but you should know that Penelope and Tara are arriving on Tuesday."

"Who are they?"

"You remember. Ava, Quinn, and I went to boarding school and college with them."

"Doesn't sound familiar, but I look forward to meeting them."

Stuart and I had talked about my friends more than once. It humiliated me that he said he had no recollection of it. My cheeks flushed, and there wasn't a damn thing I could do about it.

When the meal was over, I invited Stuart to take a walk on the beach, but he begged off, saying the cold made his knees ache.

"I'm heading back to the inn if you want a ride," offered Striker.

I prayed Stuart would decline the invitation, but he didn't.

"What time should I expect you in the morning?" he asked.

"I'll walk you out." I all but pulled Stuart through the front door. "I'll take you back," I said once we were outside. "We can talk about what you'd like to do tomorrow."

"Should we—"

"No," I answered before he could say another word about Striker. "He'll figure it out."

23

Striker

"I'd laugh if it weren't my sister-in-law on the other side of these games you're playing," said Razor, pointing out the window. "Looks like you're spared a driving companion tonight."

Ava stalked back down the hallway after putting the baby down and made a beeline straight for me. "You and I need to talk."

Razor raised his eyebrows and smirked. "You're in for it now, man," he whispered.

"Have a seat," she said with her hands on her hips.

I knew better than to argue.

Rather than sitting herself, Ava paced.

"My sister is also my best friend, Striker. The last thing I want her to do is leave, but if you keep this up, I'm going to tell her to."

"Keep what up?"

"You can't keep your eyes off her. Do you think she doesn't notice? Or that Stuart doesn't?" She shook her head. "You broke her heart. Don't you get that? Stop acting like you've changed your mind. Unless you have, you're being incredibly unfair to her."

"Are you finished?"

I heard Razor chuckle from somewhere behind me.

"You can talk," she answered.

"I care about your sister, and as I've told her countless times, I want us to be able to be friends."

The noise I heard Razor make sounded like a cross between a cough and the word "bullshit."

"Leave her alone, Striker. I mean it. What you're doing isn't funny, no matter what my husband may think."

"I'm with you, baby, all the way," said Razor.

I leaned forward and put my elbows on my knees.

"If you have something else to say, now's your chance," she said, sitting down in the chair next to me.

I shook my head. "I don't."

"What happened, Striker? Why did you break up with her?" she asked.

"I'm no good for her."

"Why didn't you give her a chance to make that decision for herself?"

"I couldn't."

"Because she would've told you that you were wrong."

I nodded and stood. "I'm going to call it a night. I'll see you both on Monday."

"Hold up, we still need to talk about your conversation with the ambassador."

"Right. Forgot all about it."

"Tell you what. We're both tired. Let's meet down in Harmony tomorrow, and you can fill me in."

"Thanks, Raze."

I walked to my car after thanking Ava for dinner, knowing every word she'd said was right. It wasn't just that I had to stop "acting interested" in Aine; I couldn't be around her at all. When I was, I couldn't help myself from watching every move she made.

Nothing would change when the plumber went home. I was hurting Aine with my behavior, not her new boyfriend.

Tomorrow I'd lay it on the line for Razor. If he wanted us to remain a team on this mission, I had to be the one calling the shots. The first change I intended to make was where we worked each day.

Instead of driving to the inn where I might run into Aine and Stuart, I went to the house in Harmony. Tonight I'd evaluate what monitoring systems were there, and since it was where Razor and I planned to meet, I might as well sleep there too.

I spent all day Saturday in Pismo Beach after I'd spoken to Razor and we decided to postpone our meeting until Monday.

"Is there anything you learned that we have to act on right away?"

"There isn't. We're still playing the watch-and-wait game for now."

Per usual, I'd slept like crap, even after getting a hotel room right on the beach last night. I finally got out of bed at eight, went for a run, came back and showered, and went out in search of breakfast.

Across the street from my hotel, I saw a diner. When I approached the entrance, the woman walking in at the same time I was, said hello.

"Hi."

"Good run this morning?"

"Uh...yeah."

"Sorry, I was out there too. I guess you don't remember seeing me."

"I had a lot on my mind."

"Are you meeting someone?" she asked when the hostess approached.

"No. It's just me."

"Do you want to share a table?"

I looked around the crowded restaurant. There was only one booth open; even the counter was full. "Sure. Okay. Thanks."

As soon as we were seated, I regretted my decision. I had zero interest in small talk or getting to know the woman seated across from me, as pretty as she was.

"Are you visiting Pismo?" she asked.

"Leaving today."

"Oh. Where's your next destination?"

"I haven't decided yet."

"Maybe I could talk you into staying another day," the woman said, her cheeks turning a sweet shade of pink.

"The truth is, I'm on a bit of a sabbatical."

She nodded, still smiling and, evidently, not giving up.

"What are you sabbating?"

I smiled. She was clever. "Women."

"Uh-oh." She laughed. "I've sabotaged you already."

"I'll get back on track when we're finished with breakfast."

"She must've done a number on you."

"She?"

"Whoever sent you on your sojourn."

"Truth is, it was me, not her."

"That's what men always say. Unless it's a divorce, and then they blame the ex-wife."

As uncomfortable as I'd been when we sat down, I found myself enjoying our conversation more than I'd expected to.

"You remind me of her," I said, surprising myself.

"Uh, thank you?"

"Yes, that's a compliment."

"In what way?"

"Do you remind me of her?"

The woman nodded. "By the way, my name is Annie."

I laughed. "Her name is very similar."

"What else? Since you didn't know my name."

"I'm Griffin, by the way."

"Nice to meet you, Griffin," she said, holding her hand out over the table.

I shook it.

"So…what else?"

There was a lot about Annie that reminded me of Aine, most of which I wouldn't feel comfortable saying. She was attractive—pretty face, killer body, smiled easily, and was funny in an intelligent way. Our conversation reminded me of the first time Aine and I met and how our conversation had been equally playful.

"You're choosing your words carefully."

"You're intuitive. So is she."

Annie looked at her menu. "It's obvious you love this woman very much."

"Is that also intuition?"

"No. It's more the look you get on your face when you're thinking about her. Talking about her too."

Once we ordered, our conversation shifted to talk about the Central Coast and didn't work its way back to Aine, thankfully. I'd enjoyed the company for breakfast, though.

When the waitress asked about separate checks, I insisted on buying Annie's breakfast.

"Thank you," she said, handing me a business card. "I cut hair in town, so if you're ever in need or want to have breakfast again, you know how to reach me."

"Thanks." I tucked the card in my wallet.

We parted ways when we left the restaurant. "It was nice to meet you, Annie," I said, waving as I walked away.

"She's a lucky woman, whoever she is."

I remembered the woman I'd told my story to on the plane had said the very same words. I doubted Aine would agree. On the other hand, if my sister hadn't died, I wouldn't have found out about her disorder and Aine and I would still be together. She didn't know it, but she was lucky that she'd dodged a bullet.

Instead of going back to Harmony or Cambria after I checked out of the hotel, I drove into San Luis Obispo. I wasn't hungry, didn't feel like having a beer, and definitely wasn't interested in shopping since all I ever noticed were things I thought Aine might like.

My phone vibrated in my pocket, and when I pulled it out, I saw Merrigan's name on the screen.

"How are you, Fatale?" I answered, using the code name she rarely used anymore.

"Better than you are, or so I've heard."

"Listen, if you're calling to lecture me about Aine, Ava beat you to it."

"Actually, I was referring to the situation in Colombia. I heard your trip was wasted."

"Not necessarily." I looked around to see if anyone was in earshot and then took a seat on a bench near the edge of the river. "I haven't briefed anyone on this yet, but my meeting with the ambassador was enlightening."

"Is this a good time to talk?"

"Not particularly. Where are you?"

"Home, in Montecito."

"Where's Doc?"

"He's here. Do you want to chat with him?"

"I could come down."

"Hold on for a moment."

I heard her muffled voice and then Doc's.

"He said it's fine."

I laughed. "He didn't say anything of the kind."

"No, he didn't, but I said it's fine, so get on the road."

"Thanks, Fatale."

"See you soon, Griff."

Aine had asked me if I was friends with all my past lovers, and the more I thought about it, I realized I wasn't. My friendship with Merrigan meant the world to me, though, especially when she recognized that tone in my voice that said I really needed to talk.

24

Aine

"I wish I could stay, but the Overleaf is my biggest customer," Stuart told me when I took him to the airport Sunday afternoon. He'd gotten a call two hours earlier, saying there was no hot water in the spa. Given Thanksgiving week was one of the biggest of the year, it would cost them thousands in lost revenue if they'd had to close that part of the resort.

"I understand," I told him, trying not to let the relief of his change of plans show. With Penelope and Tara arriving on Tuesday, I'd been stressed about how much time I'd have for them with Stuart in town too.

"I'll see if I can come back next Saturday. It won't be for Thanksgiving, but we could spend the weekend together," he said when we got out of the car and kissed goodbye at the curb.

"I'd like that, Stuart."

I watched him walk into the terminal, not sure if I was sad or relieved that he didn't turn back to look at me before he went inside.

I rolled my shoulders and took several deep breaths, letting go of the tension I'd felt since he arrived on Friday.

Thankfully, we hadn't seen Striker on Saturday or this morning.

"Tabon and Striker are meeting with Mercer in Harmony tomorrow," Ava said when I got back from the airport.

"Will Quinn be coming here?"

"She will be today. Mercer is going to drop her off in a little while. She mentioned it might be a good time to get in touch with Merrigan."

"I don't know, Ava. If I want to stay with Stuart, is it really a good idea for me to dive deeper into Striker's reasons for ending our relationship?"

Ava turned to get something out of the refrigerator.

"What?" I asked when she turned back around and didn't comment.

"I'm trying not to give you unsolicited advice."

I rolled my eyes. "Are we going to do this every time? Go ahead, and tell me what you think."

"Are you going to stay with Stuart?"

"I don't know."

"You didn't seem to be enjoying yourself."

"I was on edge all weekend, expecting Striker to show up."

"Me too."

"I'll call her. It won't seem as weird since she's married to my father," offered Quinn after Ava and I argued about whether it would be out of left field for one of us to call Merrigan. Before either of us could respond, Quinn had her phone in her hand.

When Merrigan picked up, she told her that she was putting her on speaker.

"How are you feeling?" she asked Quinn.

"Good days and bad, but I think the bad ones are coming less often."

"Me too."

Quinn put her finger in front of her lips when Ava looked at her with wide eyes.

"Um, Mer, Ava and Aine just walked in."

"Oh, hello, ladies. How are you both? You probably just figured out that I'm pregnant. So my answer is, I'm great, but I'm starting to think I'm too old for this. I should leave the next batch of wee ones to the three of you to bring into the world."

"We, uh, called to ask you about Striker," said Quinn, getting right to the point.

"Hold on a moment," Merrigan whispered. "Okay, I'm outside. What about Striker? Who, just so you know, is sitting in my kitchen."

My eyes opened as wide as Ava's had a minute ago. "Hang up," I mouthed, making a cutting motion with my hand.

"We don't want to keep you from your guest. We'll talk later," said Quinn.

"Oh no, you don't. What insider information are you trying to get on Griff?"

"Merrigan, this is Aine speaking. I'm so sorry about this. Please forget we called."

"You have five seconds to start talking. If you don't, I'll go in and tell Griff you're on the phone."

Quinn laughed and shook her head. "I should've warned you that you never say 'I'll tell you later,' to Merrigan. She'll pull it out of you if you do."

I looked between Ava and Quinn, who were obviously waiting for me to say something.

I cleared my throat. "I was wondering if you knew anything about his sister's death."

"No. I don't," Merrigan answered. Her voice had gone from a teasing lilt to sad.

"I'm sorry," I said again. "That was the only thing we wanted to know."

"I'll see what I can find out."

Before I could ask her not to, Quinn held up her phone for me to see that Merrigan had ended the call.

"Oh, God." I put my head in my hands. "What have I done? She's going to tell Striker I was asking about him."

"She won't," said Quinn. "She isn't like that."

I wrapped my arms around my stomach.

"Are you okay?" asked Quinn.

"She thinks she has an ulcer."

"You're very pale."

"That's what I said the last time this happened." Ava walked over and felt my forehead.

"Why do you keep doing that? My stomach hurts. I'd know if I had a fever." I went to sit in the living room. When I told Ava I thought I might have an ulcer, I'd been kidding. But the pain was getting worse. Maybe I should try to make a doctor's appointment. But whom would I go to here? Better to wait until I was back in Yachats and could see my primary care physician.

"Do you need to go to urgent care?" asked Ava, sitting down next to me.

I stretched out and put my legs on Ava's lap.

"I'm sure I'll feel a lot better if you give me a foot massage."

Ava pushed my legs away and sat in the chair. "There are plenty of spas in town where you can get a massage. I'm serious, though. Maybe I should take you to the emergency room."

"Actually, I'm feeling a little better. I'll probably be completely fine if we stop talking about Striker so much."

25

Striker

"Here she is," said Doc, holding his hand out to Merrigan. "Who was that?"

"Quinn, she was checking in to see how I'm feeling."

"Are you ill?" I asked.

"No. Not at all." She smiled and rested her hand on Doc's arm. "We're having another baby."

"Congratulations," I said, once again surprised by how happy news of someone having a child made me. Maybe it was just because I cared so deeply for Merrigan, but then, I'd felt similarly when Mercer announced that Quinn was pregnant.

"Thanks. I think I'm over the worst of the morning sickness at this point."

"The first trimester is the hardest," explained Doc, as though that might mean something to me.

"Tell us what you came down for," said Merrigan, winking at my unease.

"I haven't briefed anyone else yet, but I wanted to fill you both in on my meeting with Ambassador Jiménez."

"How is Santiago?" asked Doc. "I haven't seen him in years."

"He appears well."

"One would think he'd give that post up soon," said Merrigan. "I can't imagine Bogotá is an easy place for a US diplomat to be."

"No, it isn't. Particularly when one of your top advisors is a mole."

"What makes him think that?" asked Doc.

"Juan Carlos' death right before we arrived."

"Could be a coincidence. I'm surprised he wasn't killed weeks ago."

"What about this mole?" asked Merrigan. "Does he have any idea who it is?"

"Negative. I even had Diesel poke around while Ranger and I met with him, but no one stood out as suspicious."

"What about you? Any ideas?" Doc asked.

"None specifically, but if whoever it is isn't connected to the Islamic State, it's got to be someone working for either Franz or Mao."

Juan Lehrer, head of the powerful Medellín Cartel, was known as "Franz" because of his surname as well as his Germanic coloring, even though he was born in Armenia.

Carlos Deodar, head of the Cali Cartel, was often called Mao, primarily for his communist beliefs, but also because of his eerie likeness to the man the world once referred to as "Chairman."

Together they were considered to be the most dangerous of the Colombian drug barons. Their massive wealth and power enabled them to bribe government and legal officials, and buy sophisticated weaponry for their protection. Some believed their influence was so far-reaching they'd soon take over not just the government, but the military too.

Before that happened, I predicted that a bloodbath in which one emerged the victor and controlled it all, was odds-on likely.

"Do you think either of them is funding Ghafor?" Merrigan asked.

"The most obvious would be Franz, given his Armenian connection, but there is a strong case to be made for Mao."

"They aren't the only cartels in South America either," added Doc.

"No, but the amount of cash that is flowing in Ghafor's direction is staggering." I pulled the notes out from my last meeting with Mercer and gave them to Doc and Merrigan to look over.

"Holy shit," Doc muttered when he finished reading the brief.

"It's a lot more than I would've predicted."

"Is there any sign, other than the sheer amount of money, that either of the cartels is connected to the Islamic State or directly to Ghafor?" Merrigan asked.

"None."

"Let's look at it from the opposite direction," suggested Doc. "What is Ghafor planning, and why would one or both of them want him to succeed?"

"At first glance, it would be easy to think that Ghafor is arming himself for an attack on the US. But would the cartels name us as their worst enemy? Would the Islamic State? There have been as many ISIS-led terrorist attacks on the UK, France, even Colombia itself."

"We need someone on the inside," said Doc.

"With all of K19's recent activity there, who do you suggest?"

"What about Tackle or Halo?" asked Merrigan.

"What's their status?"

"On board, but without known connection to us," she answered.

I nodded. "Good. I'll make contact."

We talked about the newest operatives' backgrounds.

Tackle, who had once been the number one defensive player in division one college football, was well versed in the Middle East and would be better placed inside the embassy.

Halo, whose mother's family was Venezuelan and who had been my protégé in South American intelligence before we both left the CIA, would be the obvious choice to infiltrate one of the cartels. Which one, was the question.

"You're far too visible, Striker, with both Ghafor and the Colombians. Put Monk in as direct handler," Doc suggested. "Then decide whether Onyx and Corazón serve as more than transport."

"Prior to sending anyone in, I'd like Eighty-eight to see if he can get a better idea of where the money is flowing from. It's also imperative we find out who's heading up the fundamentalist organization as soon as possible. I don't want to make a move on Ghafor until we know."

Doc nodded. "What was Santiago's take?"

"He didn't have one."

Doc raised his eyebrow and looked at Merrigan.

"If you're asking, I agree that it's unlikely he's as disengaged as he appears to be."

"What about MI6?" I asked.

"I'll make contact and see if anyone in Colombia is on their radar," Merrigan offered. "You're aware Shiver's out? Meaning he's retired."

I nodded. "I'd also heard his brother, Wilder, was being considered as his replacement."

"It remains a rumor for now."

Both Doc and Merrigan jumped when they heard the baby's wail through the monitor sitting on the coffee table.

"I'll get him," offered Doc.

"Thanks, darling." Merrigan leaned back in her chair, looking more tired than I remembered seeing her outside of a mission.

"Are you sure you're okay?" I asked once Doc was out of earshot.

"I'm fine," she said, smiling and rubbing her belly. "I want this for you, Griff. I can't wait to see you with a baby of your own. You'll make an amazing father."

I did my best not to react, but hiding anything from Merrigan was impossible. Not only had the woman known me for years, she was also a former MI6 agent. She'd been one of the highest-ranking operatives they had until she retired to spend her life with Doc and run K19.

"Fess up, Ellis. What makes you think you never will be?"

I should've known her first strike would be right at the heart of it. "I can't."

"That could be construed in so many ways. What makes you say you can't?"

Merrigan would be the third person I told this story. The first had been a virtual stranger—someone I met on a plane. The second was Razor. Why I'd confided in him was still a mystery. And now, her. Out of anyone I knew, she would understand the best.

"I got a call earlier in the year. The man identified himself as a doctor and then told me he was calling regarding Pamela Ellis, my sister."

26

Aine

"We're going to have a houseful for Thanksgiving dinner," said Ava when I walked in with Sam in my arms.

"Mom won't be back from her cruise for another couple of weeks. Who else is coming?"

"Besides you, me, and Tabon? His mother and sister plus her two girls. That, of course, means Monk will be here."

"That's ten with Penelope and Tara."

"Tabon said that since Quinn wanted to be here too, she and Mercer talked Doc and Merrigan into coming."

"Sixteen, then, if you count their baby and Sam."

"I guess I should since they're both in high chairs. That's too many for us to all fit at the table. It's going to have to be more casual."

"No one will care, Ava."

"I know. I just wanted it to be nice."

I laughed. "What would make it nicer than the Tribe of Five being together again, plus so many other friends and family?"

Since Ava hadn't mentioned Striker, I didn't either. I was sure my sister would've if he were planning to join us. I wondered what he'd do instead, though. It wasn't as though he had any family to spend it with. Maybe he was staying away intentionally because he thought I wouldn't want him to be here.

"What about Striker?" I asked, feeling guilty.

"Right. That makes seventeen."

"So he is coming?"

"It wouldn't be very nice of us not to invite him."

I nodded.

"You're okay with it, right?"

"Absolutely."

Ava sighed. "Thank goodness." She tapped the notepad in front of her with the end of her pen. "Are you sure Stuart isn't coming?"

"Positive. The job at the Overleaf ended up being a broken water main. It's surprising that the spa was the only area without water. He said it was bad enough that it should've affected the whole inn."

Ava nodded, but I didn't think she'd been listening. Broken water mains weren't exactly hot topics of conversation—unless you were a plumber.

"I feel as though I'm forgetting someone."

"What about Zary? Are she and Gunner coming?"

Ava shook her head. "I talked to her yesterday, and she said they changed their plans and will definitely be here for Christmas, but they're staying in Maryland with her mother and his for Thanksgiving."

"I can't wait to see Lia again."

"I feel bad that we haven't been back since she was born."

Now that Ava mentioned it, I felt terrible. "We're lousy sisters."

"I feel like we should get on a plane right this minute."

"Where you off to, Avarie? And are you takin' me with you?" Tabon put his arm around my sister's waist like he did so often.

"Nowhere." She sighed. "I just wish Zary and Gunner were going to be here for Thanksgiving."

"They are."

"Wait. What? Yesterday she said they wouldn't be."

"I guess she changed her mind after she talked to you. They're flying in Thursday morning."

"I should make other arrangements for a place to stay."

"You can stay with us, although there's still plenty of room next door," said Tabon.

"I can't intrude on them."

"Hello? She's your sister as much as I am. Well, maybe not exactly."

"About that, Zary wants you to call her when you have a minute."

"I'll do that right now." I handed Sam to him.

I went out on the deck to place the call; Zary answered on the first ring.

"We were just talking about how we can't wait to see you and Lia again," I said. "We're so happy you and Gunner will be spending Thanksgiving with us."

"That's why I wanted to talk with you. Both my mother and Gunner's mother want to come too. Is that too much?"

"Not at all. We're excited to see them too."

We talked about where everyone would sleep, and I assured Zary I could stay with Tabon and Ava, so there'd be plenty of room for her mother and Gunner's.

"It's your house, Zary," I said when my half sister worried about asking me to move.

After we hung up, I stayed out on the deck. While the air was chilly, the sun was bright today and felt good on my skin.

It was hard to believe that a year ago, Striker and I were still just getting to know each other. The first time we were together had been right before Thanksgiving. I'd been so nervous, especially about sex, but he'd reassured me and made me feel as though I excited him in a way that no other woman ever had.

I wiped a tear from my cheek. I missed him so much. Not just the sex, even though it was otherworldly. I missed talking to him, spending time with him, just being near him. Every inch of my body longed to be next to his, to feel him hold me, kiss me, bring me pleasure and let me do the same for him. It wasn't that I just longed for Griffin—not Striker—I ached for him, and that wasn't fair to Stuart.

In the months after our breakup, I'd convinced myself I was over him, but now I realized I wasn't even close. Until I could say I'd truly gotten past my relationship with Griffin, I couldn't be with Stuart or any other man.

If he couldn't come down on Saturday like he was planning, I'd make arrangements to fly up to Yachats early next week and end things with him. Stuart deserved to be told in person. I hated hearing about people breaking up over the phone, or worse, via text.

My sister's screech jarred me out of my seat. When I saw Penelope and Tara through the window, I ran inside, screaming like Ava had. Before I reached my two friends, I stopped in my tracks.

"What are you doing here?" I asked Stuart, who was standing behind them.

"Nice welcome for your boyfriend," Tara said, poking me.

I hurried over and hugged him. "I'm surprised, that's all. I thought you said you couldn't make it."

"I was able to get the water main fixed and then made arrangements with Benji to be on call. It'll cost me if it doesn't hold or he gets called in on something else, but I figured it was worth it."

I smiled and rested my head on his chest when he put his arms around me. Stuart was a good man. Being with him reminded me of that. Breaking up with him just because I found myself missing Striker was silly.

"I'm so glad you're here," I said again, hugging him tighter.

"We were at the rental car counter," Tara said after I'd hugged her and Penelope, "and Stuart overheard us give the agent our names. He introduced himself, and we offered him a ride so he wouldn't have to rent a car too."

"That worked out well," commented Tabon, stepping forward to hug both of the women and shake Stuart's hand.

"So, where are we staying?" asked Tara.

With only three bedrooms in each side of the duplex, space was tight. Ava had told me she could stay with them, but maybe I should offer to let our friends stay here instead. Plus, Tabon's mother, sister, and her two daughters and Monk were coming. Where would they stay? And what about Stuart? This was becoming a logistical nightmare. Why hadn't Ava and I talked about this ahead of time?

Actually we had, now that I thought about it. I hadn't planned to stay here, and there would've been two extra bedrooms next door if Zary and Gunner weren't arriving on Thursday with both of their mothers.

"Tabon, can you check and see if the house down the road has been booked for the week?" Ava asked.

"Already did, and I have it reserved from Thursday to Sunday."

"I can stay there with Tara and Pen," I offered.

All eyes immediately settled on Stuart, who put his hands on my shoulders. "I was able to get a room at the same place I stayed last time."

"Um...okay. We can talk about it later."

Stuart nodded, but I sensed his discomfort was equal to mine.

"Who else is coming?" asked Tara. "Any hot guys I can hook up with?"

"Tara!" gasped Ava.

"Oh, please. Just because you're an old married woman doesn't mean the rest of us are." Tara looked over at me. "What about that guy you were with at Ava and Tabon's wedding?"

I'd thought I couldn't be more uncomfortable a minute ago when Stuart mentioned the room he'd booked, as though he was suggesting I stay with him, but Tara's interest in Striker mortified me. What could I say in response, though? Stuart's hands were still gripping my shoulders.

"I don't know about you, but I need to excuse myself from this conversation," said Tabon, motioning with his head.

Stuart leaned down and kissed my cheek before following my sister's husband out of the room.

"What the heck, Aine?" said Tara as soon as they were gone. "You should've seen the look on your face when I mentioned Striker. Are you seeing both of them?"

Ava stepped forward and put her hand on Tara's arm. "It wasn't an easy breakup for my sister. Maybe you could scale it back a bit."

I didn't like the look on our friend's face. Tara raised her chin as though Ava had just issued a challenge. I'd seen her in action and knew that once she set her sights on a man, she rarely failed at gaining his interest.

I would literally die if Striker hooked up with Tara, but what could I do? If I asked her not to go after him, it would lead to a conversation about Stuart and me that I didn't want to have. I had no doubt that Tara would call me out on claiming both men, and there was no guarantee she wouldn't do it in front of either of them.

"Speak of the devil," Pen said when I saw Striker walking up to the front door.

"I'll get it," Tara offered.

I looked at Ava, who rolled her eyes and mouthed, "Sorry."

27

Striker

I wasn't sure what I'd just walked into, but the tension in the house's entryway was as thick as bay area fog.

"I'm here to meet with Razor," I said when all four women looked at me.

"He's downstairs," said Ava, adding, "with Stuart," when I walked away.

Maybe that's why they were all staring at me. Did they think I'd a scene?

After my conversation with Merrigan, I was even more determined not to pull Aine into my DNA clusterfuck. She hadn't agreed, but saying the words out loud to someone who knew me as well as Fatale did, had allowed me to let my guard down and talk from an emotional place rather than just state the facts I'd shared with the stranger on the plane and Razor.

"Hey, Striker," Razor said when I walked into the workout room where he was talking to Stuart. I'd noticed when I walked by that the office door was closed.

"Hello, Stuart," I said, determined not to be as much of an asshole as I'd been the other times I was around the plumber.

The man stepped forward and shook my hand but didn't say anything.

"Is Mercer here yet?" I asked.

"Negative. Should be soon, though. I'm sure Quinn is champing at the bit to see Penelope and Tara."

"Is our meeting still on?"

"Sure is." Razor looked at the plumber. "Don't want to be rude, but today is a workday for us."

"Not a problem."

I watched Stu head up the stairs, then followed Razor into the office. "What the hell is going on?"

"What do you mean?"

"Maybe it was my imagination."

"Oh, you mean the conversation taking place upstairs?"

"Crickets when I walked in."

Razor laughed. "That's because you were the hot topic when I rescued Stuart and brought him down here."

"Me?"

"Yeah, there aren't that many of us who are still single, and you're one of the only bachelors here this weekend."

I scrubbed my face. "Fuck."

"Sorry, dude."

"Maybe I should skip Thanksgiving this year."

"No way," said Razor, surprising me with his tone of voice.

"It isn't a problem. I'm not big on holidays anyway."

"No, and that's final."

"What the hell?"

"You're not spending Thanksgiving alone, Ellis."

"Not a big deal."

"It is to me. I'll feel like shit, and if I feel like shit, Avarie will too, and if she feels like shit, everyone else here will know it."

"I don't want to cause trouble."

"Don't let Tara crawl into your bed, and there won't be any."

"Jesus. Seriously?"

"Yep, that's what they were talking about when Stuart and I left the room."

No wonder Aine looked so tense when I walked in. Was her friend really that insensitive? Didn't women have some kind of code about not hooking up with someone's ex-boyfriend? I looked over at the doorway and saw Aine standing in the hallway.

"I'm sorry to interrupt, but is Stuart down here?"

"Nope, he went back upstairs a minute ago," Razor answered.

"Oh. I didn't see him."

"Are you okay?" I asked.

"Yeah...um...can I talk to you for a minute?"

"What's up?" I led her into the workout room.

"I'm really sorry," she said.

"For?"

"What happened when you came in. We were..."

"I know. Razor told me what you were talking about."

"Like I said, I'm so sorry."

I wanted to put my arms around her, pull her close to me, and tell her she had no reason to be sorry, but that would only perpetuate the tension between us.

If only I could talk Razor into working in Harmony rather than here, but each time I brought it up, my teammate had refused, saying that the equipment we had here was far superior to what was in the other house. I wasn't sure if it was far superior enough to offset the drama I was causing by being here.

I put both hands on Aine's shoulders. "I need you to be honest with me about something."

She nodded.

"Would you like me to leave?"

When her eyes filled with tears and she shook her head, I couldn't hold back.

"Come here," I said, drawing her into my arms. "Please don't cry over me. I'm not worth it."

That only seemed to make her cry harder.

"I hate that I'm the one who makes you sad." I drew back and wiped her tears. "I don't want to make you cry, Aine."

She shook her head. "It isn't you. I'm the one who shouldn't be here. Just because my sister is married to Tabon, doesn't mean I have to be around all the time."

"Not just your sister; your best friend is married to Mercer, and your half sister is married to Gunner. Seems to me that you've plenty of ties to this group."

"I'm sorry," she said for the third or fourth time. I'd lost track of the number of her apologies.

"Stop this." I looked into her eyes. "After Thanksgiving, when things have calmed down, you and I will talk. Really talk. I haven't been completely honest with you, and I see now how unfair that is. You deserve to know the truth."

"I see, I guess that means…" Aine cried harder than she had before, pulled back, and put her hands over her face.

"Means what?"

"You said you weren't completely honest with me. Does that mean there is someone else?"

I smiled and pulled her back in my embrace. "No, Aine. There isn't anyone else, and there never will be."

"I don't understand."

"Let's not get into this now. I promise, next week, when there aren't so many people here, we'll talk."

When she rested her head against my chest, I wove my fingers into her hair. "Sweet, sweet Aine," I murmured, wishing so much that things were different.

"Am I interrupting?"

When I looked up, Stuart was standing in the doorway.

Aine pulled away as though we'd been caught doing something wrong. I wished she hadn't, because we weren't. "Stuart..."

"Would you excuse us?" the plumber asked.

"I don't want you to get the wrong idea. Aine and I are friends. That's it."

"I'd like to talk to Aine alone if you wouldn't mind."

"It's okay, Striker."

I walked out of the workout room, but didn't go upstairs. Instead, I went into the office and left the door open. If things went too far south between Aine and her boyfriend, I wanted to be close enough to intervene.

28

Aine

"I guess I shouldn't have assumed it was okay for me to surprise you."

"What Striker said is the truth, Stuart. He and I are just friends. He was comforting me over something that happened with Tara and Pen. It was nothing more than that."

"Aine, please. I know what I saw, and that wasn't a friend comforting another friend. I don't know what happened between you two, but it's obvious you still have strong feelings for each other."

I shook my head, but I couldn't say he was wrong. I'd already lied to him enough each time I told him that Striker was just someone who worked with Tabon.

"I'm sorry, Stuart."

"Walk me upstairs so I can say goodbye?"

I nodded and went in front of him. As difficult as this was, it was for the best. I'd planned to break up with him anyway, before he showed up unexpectedly. He was right that he shouldn't have assumed it was okay to surprise me, but that didn't make me feel any better about how things were ending between us.

"Stuart needs to get back," I said to Ava when we got to the top of the stairs.

"But you just got here."

"Something came up," he said, looking between my sister and me.

"I'll be back after I take Stuart to the airport."

"I can call a cab."

"In Cambria? I don't think so," said Ava. "Wait," she added, looking at me. "Are you okay? You're pale again. Go sit down."

"What's happening?" asked Tabon, coming upstairs.

"Stuart needs to go back to Yachats, but I don't think Aine should take him to the airport. Look at her."

I had to admit, my stomach hurt worse than it had any time before. I gripped the back of the sofa.

"Sit down!" Ava shouted at me.

I didn't argue. I felt like I might pass out.

"I'll give you a lift to the airport," Tabon offered.

"Thank you. I'm so sorry, Stuart."

The look of concern on Stuart's face mirrored my sister's. Did I really look that bad?

Pen and Tara came inside too.

"What's wrong?" Tara asked.

"Nothing. I have a stomach ache. Why is everyone making such a big deal of it?"

Tara walked over and felt my forehead. I tried to move out of her reach, but there wasn't any place I could go.

"You're warm. Maybe you should rest."

Sure, Tara wanted me to rest, probably so she could sink her hooks into Striker without my interference. Although he'd said there wasn't anyone else, and then he'd added that there never would be.

I rested my head against one of the throw pillows when the pain intensified. Obviously, I was right about the stress giving me an ulcer. Every time I thought about Striker, it hurt worse.

Stuart came over to the sofa, and Tara moved out of his way.

"I'm sorry," I said again when he knelt beside me.

"I'm worried about you." He ran his fingertip down my cheek. "I don't want to leave if there's something wrong."

"It's okay. I'm sure it's just a stomach bug or something like that. Better you go so you don't catch it."

He nodded, leaned forward, and kissed my forehead. The hurt look he'd had on his face when I saw him standing in the doorway, witnessing Striker comforting me, was back.

"I'm sorry," I said again.

"I'll see you when you get back?" he asked.

"Yes. Definitely."

"Thanks for including me even though I showed up unexpectedly," he said to Ava.

"It's okay. I'm sorry you have to leave, Stuart."

"Wait. What? He's leaving?" asked Tara.

"Something came up," he said a second time. "Bye, everyone."

"What was that all about?" Ava asked as soon as the door closed behind him and Tabon.

I shut my eyes, wishing I didn't have to explain, especially in front of our two friends.

"He came downstairs and saw me talking to Striker."

"So he left? That's a little extreme," said Penelope, sitting down and putting my legs over her lap. "What can I do to make you feel better?"

"I should probably go next door and see if I can sleep. I don't want to get everyone sick if this turns out to be a virus. Especially Sam."

"I'll check on you in a little while."

"Thanks, Ava. I'm sure I'll be fine. Maybe I'll try meditating." I winked at her.

"You should," she said, walking me to the front door. "When I come over later, you can tell me what Stuart's leaving was really about," she whispered.

I was feeling worse by the minute. Just walking out of one door and into the other sapped my energy.

I tried to sit up when I heard Ava's voice, but the pain had gotten a lot worse.

"Oh my God, you look even more terrible," she cried. "I'm getting Tabon."

I didn't argue. Maybe I should go to the emergency room. "Is he back from the airport?"

She nodded.

"Where are you?" I heard Tabon call out.

In here," Ava answered.

"What's going on?" he asked, walking into the room.

"Something's wrong with Aine."

"Aine, look at me." Tabon put his hand on my forehead. "You're burning up. Are you in pain?"

"My stomach." The pain got worse, and I clutched the pillow.

"We need to get you to a hospital."

When Tabon tried to pick me up, I pushed his hand away, but he grabbed my wrist.

"Your heart rate is too high; you're clammy, pale, and you have a fever. I don't want you to try to walk."

When the stabbing pains started again, I gave in. "Okay."

"You stay here with Sam," he said to Ava, who was following behind us.

She ran ahead and opened the door of the SUV so Tabon could set me inside.

"What's going on?" I heard either Pen or Tara shout. I didn't feel like opening my eyes to find out which one.

"I'm taking Aine to the hospital," Tabon answered. "Tara, please go grab a blanket and a pillow."

Penelope walked over to the SUV. "We'll follow you there."

"It's okay. I'll be okay."

"What's going on?" I heard Striker shout. Penelope stepped aside when he ran up to the SUV. "Ava said Razor is taking you to the emergency room." He put his hand on my head. "Jesus, you're burning up."

"You wanna ride along?" Tabon asked.

Striker nodded.

"Get in the back seat with her."

He went around to the other side of the SUV, got in, and put the pillow Tara handed him on his lap. "Try to lie down if you can."

"You don't have to go to all this trouble. You can stay here."

Striker didn't answer, but I didn't care. His fingers in my hair felt too good.

"I thought you were at the airport?" I heard Striker ask as Tabon pulled out of the driveway.

"I'd just gotten back when Ava texted that there was something wrong with Aine."

"Why didn't you say something?" Striker asked, his fingers still stroking my hair.

"I thought maybe I had an ulcer."

"Sweet girl," he whispered. "We'll get you to the hospital as fast as we can."

"You should call and let them know we're on the way," Tabon said from the front seat.

"Good idea."

I didn't know how much time had passed when I felt the SUV come to a stop.

"I'll be right back," Tabon said and got out.

Within seconds it seemed, Striker was lifting me out of the vehicle and onto a gurney while Tabon was telling one of the people who came back outside with him what my symptoms were.

"How long have you had this pain?" a woman asked.

"I don't know. It comes and goes. Maybe a few days."

"Any change in appetite? Weight loss?"

"She's lost at least twenty pounds," said Tabon.

"Are you her husband?" the woman asked.

"No, I'm her brother-in-law. My wife is her twin sister."

"Aine!" I heard Quinn shout, running up when they wheeled me inside. "Are you okay? What's going on? We got here as soon as we could."

"You'll need to wait outside, miss," said the woman who had been asking questions. "I'll let you know when the doctor has finished examining her."

"I'm not leaving her here alone," said Quinn. "She's my oldest and dearest friend."

"Ours too," I heard Pen and Tara add. They must've just gotten here.

The woman looked at Striker. "Who are you?"

"My name is Griffin Ellis, and if it's okay with these three ladies, I'll stay with her."

I watched the woman take her glasses off and look straight at him. "Okay, you can stay for now, but once the doctor gets here, you'll have to step outside."

"I'll keep you posted," he said, still holding my hand as they wheeled me into a room. He pulled a chair closer to the bed.

"We're going to start an IV," said a different woman who came in and introduced herself as Jenny. "We need to get you into a gown first."

"I'll help," said Striker.

"Okay, I'll be back in a minute."

I tried to sit up, but the pain was too intense.

"I'll do it." Striker gently pushed my shirt up and over my head. He removed each of my arms, taking care not to jar me too much. If I weren't in so much pain, I'd thank him, but even talking hurt.

Once he unfastened and took off my bra, he held the hospital gown up. "Put your arms through here," he said and then fastened it behind me.

Next, he unbuttoned my jeans and slid them off my body.

"Thank you."

He kissed my forehead, folded my clothes, and then sat back down in the chair.

"Knock, knock," said Jenny, pulling the curtain back. "Let's get your IV started so we can get some pain meds in you as soon as the doctor gets here."

Striker stood and moved out of her way.

"A little pinch," said the nurse as she poked me with a needle. "Allergies?" she asked, fussing with the tubes.

"I don't think so."

"Here's the doctor now," Jenny said when a man pulled the curtain back.

"I'm Dr. Stevens," he said, holding out his hand to shake mine.

I tried to move but flinched, so he patted my hand instead.

"Let's take a look and see what's causing you all this pain."

He pulled up the gown and pressed against different areas on my abdomen. When he touched on the lower right, I cried out.

"Let's start a morphine drip, and then we'll get you in for an MRI. I don't think it's appendicitis, your pain is too low, but it will tell us for sure."

Jenny came back a few minutes later with a syringe.

"This will help ease the pain while we find out what's causing it. It might burn a little."

I let my eyes drift closed as the pain medicine flowed into my body. I was so tired. The last thing I saw before I drifted off was Striker leaning down to kiss my forehead.

"Hi," said Ava.

I fluttered my eyes, trying to get them to open fully. "What's going on?" I asked, raising my head.

"You had surgery. You're in the recovery room."

"For what?"

"There was a reason your stomach hurt, sweetie. Although it wasn't really in your stomach."

"What wasn't?"

"You had a mass on your right ovary that needed to be removed immediately. It was so big that if it had burst, it might've killed you."

"What time is it?"

"A little after four in the afternoon."

"I'm sorry. I can't keep my eyes open."

"Go back to sleep, sweetie. Just let yourself rest."

When I woke up again, I was in a different room, and Ava was still by my side.

"There she is," Ava sang, just like we did when either of us went to get Sam out of his crib after a nap. "How are you feeling?"

I didn't feel much of anything except tired. I tried to roll to my side, and that's when I felt pain.

"Don't do that," scolded Ava. "You almost rolled on your incision."

"Tell me again what happened."

"You had surgery, sweetie."

"I know that part."

"The surgeon removed a large mass on your right ovary and three smaller ones on the left. He said you must've been in considerable pain. Why didn't you say anything?"

I rested my head against the pillow and closed my eyes. Ava leaned over and kissed my cheek.

When I opened my eyes again, Striker was sitting in the chair where Ava had been.

"Where's my sister?"

"Razor insisted Ava take a break. I think he took her home to spend some time with Sam."

"You don't have to stay."

"I'm not going anywhere."

I tried to shift into a position that was more comfortable but couldn't find one. Striker stood and picked up a pillow that was sitting on one of the other chairs.

"Let's try this," he said, tucking it under my right side. "Better?"

"It is. Thank you." My eyes drifted closed. "I'm sorry. I'm just so tired."

"Sleep, sweetheart," he whispered as he ran his fingers through my hair.

I remembered him doing that in the SUV on the way to the hospital.

"Why are you here, Griffin?" I whispered right before I closed my eyes.

In my dream, he told me it was because he loved me.

29

Striker

I studied Aine as she slept. How had I not realized the dark shadows under her eyes and the pained expression I caught a couple of times were indicators that something was wrong? If I had, I might've been able to convince her to see a doctor before it became an emergency.

I smoothed her blonde hair, thankful that Razor had gotten her to the hospital so quickly and that she was going to be okay.

I closed my eyes momentarily, and when I opened them, Aine was looking at me.

"You don't have to stay," she said again.

"I told you before that I'm not going anywhere."

We both turned our heads when the door opened.

"Look who's finally awake," said the nurse who set a laptop on the bedside tray table and checked the various monitors in the room.

"How would you rate your pain?" she asked.

Aine shifted to sit up straighter and winced.

"I can't help alleviate it if you don't answer me honestly," the woman scolded. She walked over and wiped a name from the dry-erase board and wrote hers instead.

"My name is Paula, and I'll be your nurse for the next ten hours. Drew, the LPN, will be helping me. Tell me, on a scale of one to ten, how would you rate your pain?"

"Seven."

The nurse pulled a cord from the side of the bed. "You can give yourself pain medication by pressing this button. It'll only allow a certain amount per hour, so if you need more, all you have to do is let me or Drew know."

I watched, but Aine didn't press the button.

"Are you hungry?" the nurse asked.

"Not really."

"I'll be back in a little while to check your incision. Oh, and I saw the doctor. He should be in shortly."

After entering a few more things into the computer, she left.

"Try to go back to sleep," I said, taking Aine's hand in mine.

"I feel like that's all I've done."

"It's what your body needs."

"Ava told me I had a mass on my ovary."

I nodded.

"That's all I remember."

"The nurse said the doctor will be in soon. I'm sure he'll answer any questions you have."

"Good."

I picked up the cord with the pain med button at the end of it. "There's no reason you should suffer. Use this, Aine."

"After the doctor has been in. I don't like feeling so out of it."

"Fair enough." I tucked the cord next to her body. "What about food?"

"I'm not hungry."

"Doesn't mean you shouldn't eat."

Aine took a deep breath and focused her gaze on me.

"Tell me what you're thinking."

"I'm wondering why you're here."

"Because I want to be."

"I can't imagine the most important thing you have to do is sit at my bedside and pester me about eating or about drugging myself up so much that I don't know what's going on."

I smiled. Feisty was good. My experience was that it was indicative of a person feeling better.

"Where's my phone?" she asked.

"I don't know." I stood and looked around, but didn't see it. I walked over to the closet and found a drawstring bag containing her belongings. When I opened it, I found both her phone and a smaller plastic bag containing her jewelry. I took the bracelet I'd given her for Christmas out, walked back over, and handed her the phone. She typically wore the bracelet on her right arm, but since that's where they'd placed the IV, I fastened it on her left wrist.

Aine looked at the bracelet and then at me.

"I like seeing it on you," I said, rubbing her wrist with my thumb. I reached into my pocket with my other hand and pulled out the compass she'd given me for Christmas. "I never go anywhere without this."

Before she could respond, the door opened and the doctor came in.

"I'll wait outside." I was about to stand when Aine tightened her grasp on my hand. I leaned in closer. "Are you sure you want me to stay?"

"Please," she whispered.

The doctor sat in one of the other chairs near the bed. "Do you remember me?" he asked. "I'm Dr. Stevens. We met in the emergency room."

Aine nodded. "I don't remember anything after that."

"You needed emergency surgery."

"Yes," she murmured with wide eyes.

The doctor looked from her to me and then down at the chart. "I didn't ask before, but are you Aine's husband?"

"A friend."

The doctor took a deep breath. "I'm afraid what I have to share with you isn't good news."

Aine's grasp on my hand tightened more.

"We weren't able to save your right ovary. The mass was too large."

Aine nodded.

"On the left side, you had several smaller cysts, which also compromised the integrity of the ovary."

"What does that mean?"

Dr. Stevens took another deep breath and looked between her and me. "I cannot guarantee that you'll be successful with any future attempts at pregnancy."

I put my other hand on top of hers.

"Do you have any questions?"

"I don't think so," she whispered.

"I need to check your incision." The doctor pulled the sheet and blanket away from her abdomen and moved the hospital gown out of his way. The area was covered by a bandage that he also removed.

Aine's eyes were closed, and a single tear ran down her cheek. I wished the doctor would hurry up so I could pull her into my arms and comfort her. I knew how much she wanted to have children. It was one of the main reasons I'd ended things with her to begin with—I knew the risk was far too great for me to be the father.

My own heart had broken at the decision I'd come to; I knew full well how she must be feeling, hearing the doctor's prognosis.

"We should have the results of the biopsy in the morning," the doctor said as he recovered her wound.

"Biopsy?" Aine asked.

"I'm fairly sure the masses were all benign, but we're running the tests anyway to be certain."

When the doctor left, Aine removed her hand from mine, adjusted the gown, and drew the sheet and blanket up. She pressed the pain button and closed her eyes.

"I need to talk to Ava," she said, opening her eyes and looking for her phone.

"Would you like me to step out while you speak with her?"

"Please."

"I'll be right outside the door."

"I'd rather you leave."

I sat down on the side of her bed. "As I told you before, I'm not going anywhere."

When I tried to take her hand again, she yanked it away and then winced with the pain the motion caused.

"I want to be alone," she said, trying to blink away the tears brimming her eyelids.

"Call Ava, and then we'll talk."

Before she could argue, I walked out of the room.

Once the door closed behind me, I called Razor.

"What's up?"

"Aine got some bad news. The doctor just told her he doesn't think she'll be able to have children."

"*Fuck*," Razor muttered. "I think Avarie's talking to her now. She'll want to come back over there."

"I figured she would. Aine just told me she wants to be alone, but I'm not leaving. I'll sit outside the door if my being in there agitates her too much."

"Appreciate it," said Razor. "I need to go. Ava's hanging up."

Since I knew Aine was no longer talking to her sister, I went back into the room. When I saw her crying, her arms wrapped around her stomach, my heart broke.

"I told you I want to be alone."

"I don't care." I closed the distance between us. This time, I didn't sit on the bed; I stretched out next to her, put my arm behind her head, and pulled her close. "Just cry it out," I said, kissing her forehead.

When Aine buried her face in my chest, I closed my eyes and rested my head against hers.

I had no idea how much time passed while I held her as she cried. When I heard the door open, I expected to see Ava. Instead, it was the plumber.

I sat up but stayed seated on the bed.

"Stuart, what are you doing here?" Aine asked.

"When I heard what happened, I caught the next plane back." The man looked at me. "Could you give us a minute?"

"Aine?"

"It's fine, Striker."

"I'll be right outside the door if you need me."

30

Aine

I watched Stuart follow Striker, making sure the door was closed tight.

"I guess he's a lot more than a friend after all."

"I got some bad news," I said, wishing I hadn't. I wasn't ready to talk to anyone other than Ava about what the doctor had told me.

Stuart sat in the chair by the bed. "What was it?"

"I know you're angry—"

"What was the news, Aine?" he repeated, louder than necessary.

"Everything okay?" asked Striker, sticking his head inside the door.

"It's okay."

Striker nodded and closed the door.

"What you saw was Striker comforting me."

He leaned forward and put his elbows on his knees. "What was the news, Aine?"

I folded my arms, not appreciating that he was demanding I talk about something I obviously wasn't ready to. Instead of answering, I scooted up straighter and pressed the button for the pain medication. I cleared my throat, giving myself another few seconds to be sure I wouldn't regret what I was about to say.

"I won't be able to have children, Stuart. The surgery...well, that's what the doctor told me."

"I see. I'm sorry, Aine."

"I'm sorry too." I waited for him to say something else, but he didn't. "I'm very tired, Stuart. I think you should go."

"I understand," he answered as he stood. "I just wanted to make sure you were okay."

"I appreciate it. I'm sorry you flew all the way back here."

"I get that things aren't going to work out with us, but it doesn't change the fact that I care about you, Aine."

"Thank you. Goodbye, Stuart."

"Goodbye, Aine."

Striker came back in before the door closed. "That was quick."

"There wasn't much to say."

He sat down on the side of the bed. "Did you tell him what the doctor said?"

"It's for the best. Having a family is important to him."

"He left because you can't have children?"

"No. I'm just saying it's for the best that we broke up."

The door opened, and Ava came in, rushing over to the bed. While she hugged me, I watched Striker walk out the door.

"I want you to tell me exactly what the doctor told you. Word for word."

31

Striker

"What the hell happened?" asked Razor, who was waiting in the hallway.

"With?"

"Stuart. What was he doing here?"

"I assumed you called him. He said he heard what happened and caught the next plane back."

"Wasn't me. How long has he been here?"

I shrugged. "Five minutes?"

"Quick visit. He blew right past me. Didn't say a word."

"When he came in, I was lying on the bed, next to Aine."

"Something you wanna tell me?"

"I was comforting her. That's all."

"Were you there when the doctor told her?"

"Yeah."

"He said she can't have children? No possible way?"

"No, not definitively. Just that the odds are against her."

"Ironic."

I wanted to tell him to just shut the fuck up.

"This changes things."

"How so?"

"She's in the same boat you are."

"It isn't the same thing at all."

"You could adopt."

"You can't be serious. What do you expect me to say? Hey, Aine. Remember what I said about not being able to be with you? That's all changed now that I know you can't have kids."

Ava came out of the room, closing the door behind her.

"How's she doing?" I asked, surprised to see her so soon.

"Miserable. She asked me to tell you to leave."

"She's already asked me herself, several times. As I told her, I'm not going anywhere."

"Her behavior made me realize something."

"What's that?"

"Is this why you ended things with her, Striker? Did you find out you couldn't have kids or decided you didn't want to?"

I glared at Razor, who shook his head. "Don't look at me."

"Why didn't you just tell her the truth?"

Before I could answer, Ava walked away.

"I didn't say a word, dude," said Razor, holding up his hands.

"I didn't say you did."

"I gotta catch up with her."

I watched Razor walk away and took a deep breath before opening the door to Aine's room.

"Why won't you leave?" she cried when I walked back over to the bed.

"I can't."

"You can." She tried to hide her tears by covering her face with her hands.

I sat on the side of the bed and took both of her hands in mine, pulling them away from her face. "Remember before, when I told you we would talk after things settled down?"

"Yes."

"I think we should do it now."

She didn't say anything, but she didn't tell me to leave again either.

"A few minutes ago, you told me you thought it was for the best that you and Stuart broke up."

Aine nodded.

"Because you know how important having a family is to him."

"That isn't why I broke up with him, Striker."

"I know that, but it's how you felt after the doctor told you that you might not be able to get pregnant."

"Where are you going with this?"

I hoped I was doing the right thing, but I'd started, so I had to finish.

"Earlier this year, I got a call saying my sister had died."

"Yes?"

"The man who called me was her doctor. Pam, that was her name, had been seeing him for about a year, trying her damnedest to get clean."

"I'm sorry, Griffin."

"I like hearing my name on your lips."

"Go on."

I took a deep breath. "He told me that, prior to that, Pam had almost overdosed. That's when he became her doctor. He said that while she was in the hospital, he ran some tests that led to him diagnosing her with bipolar disorder and schizophrenia."

I closed my eyes and looked up at the ceiling, knowing I had to force myself to tell Aine the rest.

"As you might guess, Pam later relapsed, and it was finally too much for her body to take."

"You don't have to go on. I can tell this is very hard for you to talk about."

"I haven't told you the most important part. He asked me if I'd ever been tested. I told him that I hadn't, and he suggested I might want to."

Aine tightened her grip on my hands.

"He went on to say that in the year he treated Pam, he found out quite a bit about our family, and while he couldn't be certain, his guess was that our mother suffered from the same illnesses."

"Did you do as he suggested?"

"I didn't."

"Why not?"

When Merrigan asked me the same question, I hadn't told her the truth, even though I was sure she'd guessed it. "I'm afraid," I whispered.

Aine moved over. "Lie next to me."

When I lowered my body next to hers, this time, Aine comforted me.

I raised my head when I heard the door open.

"Sorry, I'll come back later," I heard Ava say and felt Aine nod.

"It's okay if you need to talk to her."

"I need to talk to you, Griffin."

I studied the brave woman lying next to me. "Go ahead, Aine. Say what you need to say. Or ask what you want to ask."

"Is this why you ended our relationship?"

"Yes."

"Because you didn't think I'd understand."

I looked into her eyes. "I'm not sure you do now. It's believed that there is a genetic predisposition for the disorder my sister suffered from, and maybe my mother too."

"Which is why he suggested you get tested."

"Yes, but not for the disorder, for the genetic variations that contribute to it."

"Did he say what the chances were that you have those variations?"

"Only that the risk of developing the condition is greater for first-degree relatives of affected individuals. That would mean both my sister and mother."

Aine was quiet for a long time, but I waited. I wanted to give her time to think, not bombard her with medical statistics.

She blinked, and a tear ran down her cheek. "I do understand, Griffin. You weren't worried about yourself."

"Not as much as I was worried about you."

"And the children you knew I wanted to have."

"I'm not telling you this now because anything has changed, Aine. I still have the same fears, the same concerns."

"Why *are* you telling me, Griffin?"

"I wanted you to understand. I wanted you to know it was nothing you did."

"That's why you said there'd never be anyone else."

"Yes."

"You're choosing to be alone for the rest of your life because of something you don't even know you have?"

"I'm choosing not to subject another person to it if I do. There is always the chance that the disorder will manifest itself in me. Just because I haven't had symptoms of it yet, doesn't mean I never will."

"Would the test tell you?"

I nodded.

"I understand why you wouldn't want to take it."

"You do?"

"In one of my classes, we talked about something similar. If there was a test that could tell a person that they were predisposed to dementia, for example, would that person want to know?"

"Would you?"

Aine took a deep breath. "I don't know."

"Same for me. I've gone back and forth trying to decide if it would be better to know or let myself remain ignorant."

"There is treatment for bipolar disorder though, right?"

"There is."

"It isn't the same as it would be if it were something like Parkinson's or Alzheimer's."

"I've considered that. So, you think I should do it?"

Aine brushed my lower lip with her thumb. "I can't answer that."

"You can tell me what you think. I'm asking."

"I can't answer, because I don't know."

"I understand."

"There is something I do know."

"What's that?"

"I want to be with you, Griffin. I don't care if we never know. I still want to be with you."

"I knew you would feel that way. It's the reason I didn't tell you."

"But now you did."

"It doesn't change the fact that I want to protect you from this."

"Let me ask you a question. What if you did do the testing and found out you didn't have the genetic variation? Would you still want to be with me, knowing I might not be able to have children?"

I knew she'd ask that question, and when I thought about it earlier, I'd had a different answer than I had now. Before, I would've told her it wasn't the same thing. Now I understood that she wouldn't see it that way. To her, it was exactly the same.

“If there were a way I could be with you, Aine, I would do it.”

“There is a way. All it takes is for you to want it.”

“What if…”

“We face it together. No matter what ‘ifs’ there are in our lives, we face them together.”

32

Aine

"Tsk, tsk, tsk. You know you can't be sleepin' in Miss Aine's bed," said the man I guessed was Drew.

Griffin—because I could no longer think of him as Striker—stretched and sat up. "What time is it?"

"Almost ten, and little miss here needs her rest, which she can't do with you hoggin' half her bed."

He stood. "Is Ava still here?"

"No, she left about an hour ago. Told me to tell Miss Aine that she'd be back in the morning."

"Oh."

"It's okay," I told him. "You can leave. I'll be sleeping anyway."

He shook his head.

"Seriously, Griffin. Go get some sleep and come back in the morning like Ava is."

"Or I could arrange to have a rollaway brought in. That way you could both sleep without having to share a little bitty bed that's barely big enough to hold one person, let alone two."

"That would be great," he answered before I could protest. "Thanks, Drew."

"Here," he said, handing him a piece of paper. "Order some food for Miss Aine and something for yourself too." Drew pointed to the bottom of the paper. "There's the number. Just call, and they'll bring it up in about thirty minutes."

"Can you eat?" Griffin asked.

"It doesn't matter. She has to. You were sleepin' in her bed; you darn well better know what she likes to eat."

I laughed, and even though it hurt, it felt good too. "Can I get breakfast?"

"You can get whatever you want," Drew answered.

"I want pancakes."

"That does sound pretty good. Maybe I'll have pancakes too."

"What you waitin' for?" Drew handed Griffin the phone. "The sooner you call, the sooner the food gets here."

"He's a character," Griffin said once Drew left the room.

"He's great."

"Yeah, I agree."

Griffin ran his hand through his hair and sat down in the chair.

"You look so tired. I'm telling you, I'll be okay if you want to go back to Cambria and sleep in a real bed."

"I won't be."

"I don't understand."

"I won't be okay."

At first I thought he was teasing, but the look on his face told me differently. Griffin had held everything he told me inside for eight months. Now that it was out in the open, he was feeling vulnerable. I wished the hospital bed was big enough for both of us. I'd sleep a lot better with him beside me too.

"You can stay, but you have to promise me that you'll take a break from this place tomorrow when Ava gets here."

"We'll see."

33

Striker

I woke up when the monitors in the room started beeping. "Aine? Are you okay?"

The door flew open; Paula, Drew, and two other people ran in.

"You need to wait outside," Drew said, dragging me by the arm.

"What's happening?"

"She's seizing."

"What does that mean?"

"She's having a seizure," Drew shouted, running back into the room.

I pulled my phone out of my pocket and called Razor. I had no idea what time it was, but it didn't matter, I had to tell Ava.

"What's up?" Razor answered.

"Aine had, is having, a seizure."

"We'll be right there."

I paced outside of Aine's room, terrified. I didn't remember saying a prayer since Aunt Dorothy used to force me to before bed, but I said one now, begging God to keep Aine alive.

Two more people rushed past me; they looked like they might be doctors. Drew came out shortly after they went in.

"She's okay," he said.

"What happened?"

"It's rare, but anesthetics can sometimes cause seizures. The doc isn't sure that's it, so he's going to run some tests."

"Can I see her?"

"Give them a few minutes to make sure she's stable, then you can go back in."

"Thanks, Drew."

The nurse slapped my back when he walked away. "Hang in there, man."

I checked my phone. It had been fifteen minutes since I called Razor, so they should be arriving any minute.

Selfishly, I hoped I'd get to go in and see Aine before they got here. Otherwise, I'd let Ava go in first, and I wanted to see that she was okay with my own eyes.

The remaining five people who had been in the room with her filed out. Paula was the last of them. "You can go in."

I rushed in and over to Aine's bedside. "How are you doing?"

"I have a headache, but otherwise I'm fine. They said I had a seizure."

"Do you remember anything?"

"Nothing. I fell asleep, and when I woke up, I was surrounded by people holding me down."

"Drew said the doctor is going to run some tests."

"What time is it?"

I looked up at the clock. "Midnight."

"God, I'm so sorry. You should go now. Seriously, Striker, get some sleep."

"Striker?"

Aine smiled. "Sorry. Griffin, go get some sleep."

"Not a chance in hell," I said, stroking her forehead. "I was so worried."

"I'm okay," she whispered.

The door flew open, and Ava ran in, followed by Razor.

"I'll warn you now that Penelope and Tara are right behind us."

I nodded.

"Wanna get a cup of coffee?" Razor asked.

"Give me a sec."

I walked over to the bed and leaned down to brush her lips with mine.

I looked at Ava. "Text Razor if she needs me."

I sat outside Aine's room, nursing my coffee.

"Did you tell her?" Razor asked, yawning.

"Yeah. How'd you know?"

"You aren't as tightly wound as you've been the past couple of weeks."

"It could just be because I'm almost sleepwalking."

"Nah. But if you need to get some rest, go back to our place. I'm sure Ava isn't going to leave her sister's side. We'll be here."

"Can't."

"I get that."

"Should we call Peggy?"

"Avarie tried. Their mother is on a cruise somewhere. I can't remember where she said. Anyway, she left a message for her."

I yawned like Razor had. "I love her, you know that, right?"

Razor rubbed my shoulder. "I knew it before you did."

The door opened, and Penelope and Tara walked out. "We're going back to the house, and Quinn is leaving too. Good luck getting Ava out of there, though."

"She can stay as long as she wants," said Razor. "Why would I want to go home and go back to bed?"

"Where's your baby?" I asked.

"Damn—we forgot all about Sam." Razor laughed and squeezed my shoulder. "Don't worry, my mom and sister are at the house. Awful paternal of you to ask, though."

"Just wanted to make sure you didn't leave him in the car."

"That isn't remotely funny," fumed Tara. "Do you know how many babies die from—"

Razor held up his hand. "You can blame our lack of sensitivity on a similar lack of sleep."

"Or we can just blame it on you being men."

"That's right. We're Neanderthals. Every one of us."

"Let's go." Penelope yawned as she pulled Tara in the direction of the elevator. "See you guys later."

I held up my hand in what might be construed as a wave, but I was so tired, I didn't do much more than raise it.

"They brought a rollaway bed in for me. I sure would like to be lying on it right now."

"What's stopping you?"

"Your wife is in there."

"So? I'm sure all they're talking about is you."

I got up and pushed the door open.

"I was just leaving," said Quinn, waving me into the room. "Call me if you need me."

"Am I interrupting?"

"Not really. We were just talking about you."

"See?" said Razor, punching my arm. "Striker here wants to go to bed, Avarie."

"But they're taking Aine for tests."

"Which they won't have the results of until tomorrow," Aine told her sister. "Go home and sleep."

"Okay, but only because he's here," Ava said, pointing at me. "Good night," she added, kissing her sister's cheek. "I'll be back in the morning. I guess it is morning. I'll be back later this morning."

Aine laughed. "You're delirious. Get out of here."

"Can you sleep?" I asked once Ava and Razor were gone.

She nodded. "What about you?"

"Only if I do this." I moved the chair away from the bed and put the rollaway in its place. "I need to be closer to you."

I stretched out as much as I could, seeing it was designed for a person half my size. I'd told Aine I could sleep if I was near her, but only because then she'd let herself do the same. I couldn't, though. I bent my elbow and rested my head on my hand, watching her.

Indecision warred inside me. Was I right to have told her the real reason I ended our relationship? It wasn't as though anything had changed. And if I did go ahead with genetic testing and it turned out I had the variations my sister had, what then?

I never thought of myself as a selfish man, but when it came to Aine, I wanted to be. I wanted to let illness and disorders and inabilities to have children be damned, and spend my life with her.

Imagining what that would be like, I rested my head on the pillow and let myself sleep.

34

Aine

I held my breath, hoping I could will the nurse away who would soon walk through the door and wake Griffin. I knew the minute his eyes opened, his face would close on the peace and serenity he exhibited only when he slept.

Instead of nightmares, his dreams this morning must be filled with the light and love he'd never allow himself to accept when the sun rose on the day ahead.

I loved the man sleeping in the too-small bed by my side. Nothing would change the way I felt, even if he remained intransigent in his determination to do what he believed was best for me rather than what was best for my heart.

Instead of being jarred awake by an overzealous hospital employee anxious to complete the first of her daily tasks, Griffin's eyes opened slowly and settled on mine.

"Good morning," he said, shielding his eyes from the stream of sunlight illuminating the room.

I smiled. "Good morning."

He smiled too. "I'd give anything to know what you're thinking."

"Trying to keep the day at bay."

He turned to his side and propped himself up on his elbow. "What are you worried about?"

"I don't know where to begin."

He sat up then and reached out for my hand. "I'm sorry, sweetheart."

Unexpected tears filled my eyes. He had no idea that his apology would only be one of many if my fears were realized. If he left me today, repeating that nothing between us had changed, my fractured heart would break in two.

"Hey," he said, standing and sitting by my side, on the bed. "Talk to me."

I shook my head, unable to speak my greatest worry.

"The doctor said he was confident the masses were benign," he said, trying to guess the reason for my tears.

I squared my shoulders and took a deep breath. "I'm okay."

"No, you're not."

"More effects of the anesthetic."

Griffin shook his head. "Tell me the truth, Aine."

The tears I'd demanded away, returned, flooding my eyes. "Don't leave me," I whispered.

Griffin cupped my cheek with his palm, leaned forward, and kissed me. "Even if you're better off without me?"

"Never," I murmured. "Never leave me again."

"You know what I do for a living."

"That isn't what I mean. Don't make me live without you, Griffin."

"Do you know what you're asking? Or better put, what you're agreeing to by asking me to stay?"

"I don't care."

"I know better."

"What if I'm the reason we can't have a family? What if it isn't you? Would you leave me then?"

"Never."

"Then, don't force me to do what you wouldn't."

His eyes remained fixed on mine as though he was searching my soul, looking for the slightest hesitation.

I put my hand on the back of his neck and pulled him closer so my lips rested just below his earlobe. "I love you, Griffin."

He pulled back, but only so far that his lips could cover mine. He kissed me deeply, one hand gripping my arm, the other still cupping my cheek.

With his forehead rested against mine, he uttered the words I'd feared I never would hear. "I love you, Aine."

I kissed him the same way he had me, holding him tight and vowing silently never to let him go.

The door opened, and Striker ended our kiss, but the spell between us remained solidly in place.

"Good morning, lovebirds," said the nurse I recognized from the afternoon before, but I couldn't remember her name.

"I'm Elizabeth," she said in a South African accent, erasing Paula's name from the board and adding hers back in its place.

Maybe it was the voice I remembered more than the face.

"Ken will be working with me today. He's next door, but he'll come over shortly and take you for your first walk of the day. The more you walk, the sooner you can go home."

Elizabeth set the same laptop Paula had used the night before on the bedside tray. She checked the monitors, pounding her thick fingers on the keyboard. She moved the blanket and sheet away, checked the incision, and then put her hands on her hips. "How badly do you want to go home for Thanksgiving?"

"Will I be able to?"

The nurse slid a piece of paper toward her. "If you can check off each of the milestones on this list, you will."

I studied the paper. All but one seemed surmountable. *No seizure* was the only thing out of my control.

I looked up at Griffin, who was reading over my shoulder.

"You can do it," he whispered.

"The doctor will be in shortly. Start working on that list," Elizabeth said before leaving the room.

"It says you have to eat," said Griffin, picking up the room's phone. "What sounds good this morning?"

I rattled off most of the breakfast menu.

"You're hungry."

"Starving," I said, wondering if he knew my hunger had nothing to do with food. I craved Griffin's naked body next to mine. Only that could satiate me.

He leaned forward and kissed me. "Let's get you out of here."

When the door opened again, I expected the doctor but saw Sam in my sister's arms instead.

"Oh, sweet boy," I cried, so happy to see my nephew.

"I had a battle with a South African Amazon over bringing him in here, but I won out."

I shook my head and scooted over so Ava could sit on the bedside. "You can't hold him. That's the caveat."

Sam, who usually reached for me immediately, stayed on his mother's lap without fussing, as if he knew he might hurt me if he didn't.

"I miss you, baby boy," I said, leaning forward to kiss his cheek.

Sam gripped my neck and brought his sweet little mouth to my cheek.

"He misses you more."

I looked up at Griffin. The look on his face was the same as it had been before he opened his eyes earlier—peace and contentment.

"Tabon's outside," Ava said. "He asked me to send you out."

"He can come in."

"It's okay. I'll be right back." Griffin kissed my cheek. When he did, Sam reached for him. He leaned closer, and the baby touched his cheeks with his lips like he had mine.

"Oh. That is so sweet. Sam gave you a kiss."

35

Striker

My face was wet with baby drool, but I didn't wipe it away until I was through the door and out in the hallway. I saw Razor a few feet away, on the phone, and he didn't look happy.

"What's up?" I asked when he turned around.

"I'm sorry to do this now, but we need to go back to the house."

"Okay." I studied Razor's face. Whatever it was, was important. "Let me tell Aine."

Razor nodded. Behind him, though, I saw the doctor approaching.

"I need to hear what he says first," I added, motioning with my head.

"There's time."

"You wanna come in too?"

He shook his head. "I have some more calls to make."

I followed the doctor through the door and met Ava coming out.

"Where's Tabon?" she asked.

"Over there."

"I'll be right back," she said, walking toward her husband. "She wants you to go in."

"The masses were benign," I heard the doctor say as I walked over to Aine's bedside.

She looked relieved, maybe more when I held her hand than by the doctor's words.

"What about the seizure?" I asked.

"The MRI will tell us more, but I suspect it was an isolated incident."

"When can I leave?"

"As long as you've done everything else on the list, I'll release you in the morning. I do want to keep you here one more night, as a precaution."

Aine nodded. Her sister had crept back into the room, but it didn't seem like she noticed.

"Any other questions?"

She started to shake her head, but stopped. "Just one. Are there tests that will tell me whether my ovary is functioning?"

"There are, but there's no point taking them for at least six weeks. By then we should be able to tell whether your body has resumed functioning normally."

Aine looked up at me. "Do you have any questions?"

"I don't," I said, unsure if I was missing something she wanted me to say.

"Elizabeth said your incision looked fine, so I don't need to check it again. I'll see you later, once we have the results of your MRI."

The doctor left the room, and Ava came back over to Aine's bedside. "I'm going to stay," she said, looking at me.

"Right." I leaned down to kiss Aine's cheek. "I need to leave, but I'll be back as soon as I can."

She moved so she could kiss me. "As much as I know I should tell you not to, to get some rest instead, I want you here too."

"Soon as I can," I repeated.

Razor was a few feet away, but instead of being on the phone, he was talking to his son.

I'd spent eight months denying that having a child was something I wanted in my life, but now I wondered what it would feel like to hold my own baby in my arms, one Aine and I made together. And if we couldn't, one we adopted together.

"Are you okay?" Razor asked. "Bad news?"

"No, good news. If all goes as planned, Aine should be able to leave the hospital tomorrow, in time for Thanksgiving." I didn't like the look on Razor's face. "What?"

"We may need you to leave."

"What? Dammit. No."

"Like I said earlier, let's head back to the house, and you can judge for yourself."

I studied the monitor, watching as the arms Ghafor had been stockpiling were being systematically transported away from his compound.

"When's the last time you laid eyes on Abdul?" I asked Monk.

"A little over eight hours ago."

"Tell him where," prompted Razor.

"Colombia."

"Where are Tackle and Halo?" Razor asked.

"Still on the East Coast. So are Onyx and Corazón," answered Monk.

With Ghafor in Colombia, there was no point in sending the team in. Neither Tackle nor Halo would have time to work their way into the embassy or one of the cartels. That level of infiltration would take weeks if not months.

"Let's keep everyone on standby for now."

"Roger that," responded Monk.

Razor motioned me out of the room. "You can head back to the hospital if you want."

"I need a shower," I muttered to myself.

"Yeah, you do."

"Fuck off."

36

Aine

"I feel like so much has happened since you and I have had a chance to talk," said Ava.

"Like what?"

"Uh, you had a seizure, and *something* happened with you and Striker. Did he tell you about his sister's death?"

I nodded. "I don't remember anything about the seizure, but I can tell you about his sister."

"What happened?"

"He got a call from her doctor after she died."

"I figured it was something like that. So what now?" Ava asked after I told her that the doctor had recommended Griffin get tested to see if he carried the same genetic defect his sister had.

"I don't know yet. I mean, I think he should do it so he knows, but I can't say for sure that I would if the situations were reversed."

"What about the seizure?"

"The doctor said I'd be going for an MRI. I don't know when, though."

The door opened again, and Pen and Tara walked in, followed by Quinn a few minutes later.

"Is it okay that we're here?" Pen asked.

"Why wouldn't it be?" I asked.

"You had a seizure. Have you forgotten that already?"

Ava looked over her shoulder to make sure the door was closed. "The seizure isn't even the big news, girls. Ask her about Striker."

I smiled. "I feel like we're back at boarding school. Any second the dorm monitor is going to walk through that door and tell us to go back to our own rooms."

"So, what happened?" Quinn asked.

"Sorry, Tara," Ava said, poking her, "but I'm pretty sure Striker is off the market."

"Damn. Who else you got?" said Penelope, poking Ava like she'd done to Tara.

"There aren't many single men left on Razor's team."

"Both Tara and I want one." Pen winked. "These spy guys are hot."

"Time for your MRI," said a man who came in with a clipboard in his hand.

"I'm going too," said Ava. "See you later, ladies."

When the orderly wheeled me back into the room after my test, Pen, Tara, and Quinn were still there, waiting.

"How did it go?" Quinn asked.

"The tech said Aine should hear something from the doctor this afternoon," Ava answered for me.

"So, where's your boyfriend?" asked Penelope.

"Which one?" Tara asked before I had a chance to respond.

"That's enough, Tara," said Ava, scowling at her.

"What? It's hard to keep up, that's all."

"Tara, quit it," said Pen.

Quinn didn't say anything, but she didn't look any happier than Ava or Penelope did.

I didn't think the snarky comments were worth responding to, so I didn't. I rested my head against the pillow and closed my eyes, wondering when Griffin would be back.

"You need to eat something," said Ava.

When I opened my eyes, my sister was looking over the menu, but Tara was looking at me.

"Do you have something else to say?" I asked directly.

Tara shook her head and folded her arms.

"Okay, then," said Quinn, standing. "Time to go, Tara."

"Why is everyone on my ass?" she asked, not making a move to get up.

"Because you're being a bitch," answered Pen, looking at her fingernails rather than at Tara. "I agree, it's time to go."

I didn't care why, but Pen's words made our friend stand when Quinn's hadn't.

Tara walked toward the door, but Pen came over and kissed my cheek. "I'd say we'd come back later, but I don't think that's a good idea."

"What's wrong with her?" I whispered.

"Not sure, but I'll see if I can find out."

"What the hell?" said Ava once our two friends had left the room.

"Something's up," said Quinn, who was usually the first to say we should reserve judgment and the last to offer an opinion.

"She's always been a bitch, but it seems like she's gotten worse."

I looked back and forth between my sister and Quinn. Both seemed concerned, but I wasn't. I had my own problems to worry about, and I'd stopped caring what Tara thought about anything.

"Do you need to rest?" Ava asked, stroking my forehead.

I closed my eyes and nodded, wishing that Griffin would walk back in the door, take me in his arms, and tell me everything would be okay. Right now, something was telling me it wouldn't be, and I hated the feeling of dread that had settled in my stomach when he left earlier.

"I'll head out too, honey," said Quinn. "You need your rest."

"Get some sleep," Ava said once Quinn was gone. "I'll be here when you wake up."

I closed my eyes and turned my body away from her so Ava wouldn't see my tears. If she asked, I wouldn't have been able to tell her why I was crying.

37

Striker

I drove to the inn on Moonstone Beach, parked, went inside the room, and sat on the bed. I was exhausted physically, mentally, and emotionally.

A few hours ago, all I'd cared about was being by Aine's side. I'd still feel that way if Ghafor was continuing to stockpile arms in Pakistan and hadn't shown up in Colombia.

Knowing I might have to leave the country soon, I cursed the job I'd always loved, but now grew to hate more with every mission. I got up and turned the shower's water to scalding before climbing in.

On my way to the hospital, I called Merrigan.

"Did you hear Ghafor is back in Colombia?" I asked.

"I hadn't. Why do you think he returned?"

"No idea, except the arms are shipping out too."

"Do you want to talk to Doc?"

"I probably should. I'll give him a call."

"Not necessary, he's right here."

"What's up?" Doc asked.

I repeated what I'd just told Merrigan and then asked how well he knew Jiménez.

"Not very. I met him years ago when he was a junior senator from New Mexico. Why?"

"His behavior when I met with him was off. As Merrigan said, I don't think he's as disengaged as he's pretending to be."

"You're the lead on this mission, Striker. You have to go with what you believe is the best course of action."

"For now, I say we continue to wait and watch."

"Roger that. On another subject, how's Aine?"

I gave him the condensed version. "If all goes well, she'll be out tomorrow."

"Just in time for Thanksgiving. Merrigan and I look forward to seeing her. Let her know that."

"Will do." I thanked him again before I hung up.

Before I went up to Aine's room, I called Razor and filled him in on my conversation with Doc.

"I told him that I want to stand down for now."

Something in my gut was telling me that Jiménez was somehow involved with Ghafor and the Islamic fundamentalists, but I couldn't piece together why or what that had to do with the arms being stockpiled.

"What about the arms?" Razor asked as though he was reading my mind. "Should we stop them in transit or keep the mission going?"

We had to keep it going. If the weaponry didn't arrive wherever it was headed, Ghafor would shut down and likely ghost, at least temporarily.

"Let the shipments go," I answered, standing up straight. "But tell Monk to keep his eyes on them and on Ghafor."

"Roger that. I will when I see him," said Razor. "By the way, are you back at the hospital?"

"Affirmative."

"Can you do something for me?"

"Anything," I said, meaning it sincerely.

"Send my wife home."

"You got it."

38

Aine

I held my breath when I heard the door open like I had every other time I'd prayed Griffin would walk in and it ended up being someone else.

I let out a sigh of relief when he came in, flowers in hand and a smile on his face.

"You're needed at home," he said to Ava as he walked past, set the flowers on the window ledge, and leaned down to give me a kiss.

"I'm waiting for the doctor to tell us the results of the MRI."

"We'll call you," I told her, not turning my head away from Griffin.

"All right, all right. I'll leave."

"Bye," I said, still looking into Griffin's eyes.

He looked up when he heard the door close.

"Is she gone?"

"Yes," he answered, laughing.

"Kiss me." I pulled him down so I could reach his lips.

"I guess you missed me."

"Every minute."

When Griffin pulled a chair over to the bed, I teared up.

"What's wrong?"

"You tell me. You seem anxious."

He shook his head. "Everything's fine."

I raised a brow.

"There's a situation in Colombia that may necessitate my leaving."

"You were just there."

"I was," he said, combing his fingers through my hair.

What could I say? This was his life. If we ended up being together, I'd have to get used to it, just like my sister had to.

"I'm here now, though."

"I'm so glad. I wish you could take me home."

"Yeah? What would we do?"

I could feel the heat in my cheeks.

"Tell me, baby," he whispered, and they got hotter.

I grasped his hand, pulled back the blanket and sheet, and rested it on my breast. "Touch me."

Griffin took a deep breath and raised my hospital gown. "Someone could come in," he said, coming around to the other side of the bed so his body would shield mine from the door.

"Leave it," he said when I went to lower the gown. "Let me look at you."

His eyes burned into my skin as his fingers toyed with my nipples. I wove my fingers in his hair and arched my back when he lowered his head and put his lips where his hands had been.

When he raised his head and lowered my gown, I groaned.

"Soon," he whispered, kissing each of my fingertips.

"Promise?"

He smiled. "Oh, yeah."

"I didn't...Stuart...we never..."

"Shh. I know."

I put my hands on either side of his face and deepened our kiss.

It didn't matter that my body was sore from the surgery; the pain of longing for him was worse. "Promise me you won't leave before we can be alone."

"We're alone now, pretty girl."

"You know what I mean."

Griffin's eyes were hooded and his breathing labored. "I want to hear you say it."

"I need to feel you inside me."

He gripped my cheeks like I'd done to him a moment ago and kissed me. "I need to love you," he whispered. "Let me love you, Aine."

39

Striker

It took every ounce of restraint I could muster not to lock the door and strip Aine bare. We'd have to wait until she'd healed before I could give her what she wanted, but there were so many other things I could do to her in the meantime. I'd trail my lips over every inch of her body until she was ready to scream my name in pleasure. I'd bring her to the brink of an orgasm, pull her back, and take her right back to the edge until she begged me to let her finish. I would, then, because I'd know that it was so much more powerful than it would've been if I'd let her fly all the other times.

"I know what you want, but I'm going to give you what you need, Aine," I told her so many times. She'd cry; she'd plead, and she'd beg, but I wouldn't relent until I was certain I'd pushed her as far as she could go. There was so much more I wanted to show her, do to her, and I would, as soon as her body could take it.

I adjusted my jeans and nipped her lower lip when she giggled. "You just wait," I warned.

"I'm already there," she said, no longer smiling. "I need you, Griffin."

"Soon, baby. I promise."

"I need you now." She grabbed my wrist and pulled it under the blanket until I touched her sex. "Please," she begged.

I let my fingers rest against her. Stroking her softly. "You aren't ready for this," I said, biting at her nipple through the hospital gown.

"I need it. Don't make me wait."

My fingers went where she wanted them, and I gave her what she asked for. Slowly, softly, gently, but that's all it took. Within seconds, she drenched my fingers as her hands gripped my arm, holding it in place, wringing all the pleasure she could from me.

We both jumped at the sound of the door opening, but rather than jerk my hand away, I slowly removed it from under the blanket and clutched her fingers.

"Good news on your MRI," the doctor said, looking between us. "Nothing abnormal showed up. As long as you have a good night, you can go home tomorrow morning."

"That's wonderful," said Aine, clutching my other hand.

"What time?"

"I'll be in early for rounds, so I'd say around ten. Again, as long as you have an uneventful night."

The doctor eyed our clasped hands and shook his head. "See you in the morning."

"Are you going to stay?" Aine asked after the doctor walked out.

"If you want me to."

"I know I'm being selfish, and I'm sure you'd sleep much better in a real bed, but..."

I smiled and ran my finger over her bottom lip. "I never sleep better than when I'm with you. Real bed or not."

She kissed the fingers I knew carried her scent. "I love you, Griffin."

"And I love you, Aine."

"Why are we stopping here?" Aine asked me the next morning when I pulled into the parking lot of Cambria Shores Inn.

"I want you all to myself for a couple of hours."

Aine smiled, and her warmth settled on me like a blanket. "It's Thanksgiving."

"It is, and your sister's place is a madhouse. She told me what time she's serving dinner and insisted that we not show up until thirty minutes prior."

"I feel bad that I'm not helping."

"Because preparing a Thanksgiving dinner for thirty people is just what the doctor ordered. Come on, let's go inside."

I came around to the other side of the car and helped her out. "What's your pain level, baby?"

"Five?"

"Tell me the truth."

"What makes you think I'm not?"

"The fact that you posed it as a question."

"Okay. It's a six."

"Right."

I opened the door to the room and flipped the switch for the fireplace. I'd made arrangements for the innkeeper to stock the room with fresh fruit, muffins, different types of cheese, two baguettes, and a pitcher of lemonade. The final item on the list was because Aine had told me she'd been craving it.

I pulled back the comforter and motioned for her to get into bed.

"All I've done is lie in bed," she protested.

"Uh-huh."

She sat down and crossed her arms.

"Take off your clothes, Aine," I said without turning around to look at her. When I could see her bring her sweater over her head out of the corner of my eye, I faced her, loving the grin on her face. Since she didn't look as though she was struggling, I let her finish while I cued up a movie on the television.

"You too," she said when I approached the bed.

"Have you forgotten I make the rules?" I smiled when her eyes drifted closed and her cheeks turned pink.

"I haven't forgotten anything." Her voice was as thick with desire as I felt.

"You heard the doctor, baby. He said that he'd let you know at your three-week checkup when you can resume 'normal activities.'"

By the way Aine's eyes drooped, I doubted she'd argue. As much as she thought she wanted more, what she really needed was rest.

By the time I was stripped down to my boxer briefs, she was asleep. I crawled into bed next to her, drew her into my arms so her cheek rested near my heart, and ran my fingers through her hair. Just feeling her bare skin on mine was enough. There was a time I couldn't have fathomed ever having that pleasure again.

My vibrating phone on the bedside table jarred me awake.

"Hello?" I answered without bothering to see who was calling.

"Sounds like I woke you," said Razor.

"Aine fell asleep." I eased my arm from under her head and went into the bathroom so I didn't wake her. "I guess I did too. What's up?"

"Ava asked me to tell you that we'll bring dinner to you."

"She isn't going to like that."

"Sometimes you have to give her what she needs over what she wants."

I laughed. "I'm pretty sure I said those very same words earlier today."

"We'll be by after we're done eating. Let her sleep in the meantime."

"Thanks, Raze."

"Take good care of her, you hear me?"

"Always."

When I came back to bed, Aine sat up and rubbed her eyes. "Who was that?"

"Your brother-in-law. He wanted me to tell you that they're bringing dinner here."

"Wait. What? What time is it?"

"A little after three."

"Oh, no! Dinner is in an hour." She tried to push me out of her way, but I wouldn't budge. "What are you doing? We have to leave."

"We aren't going anywhere."

"But..."

I raised a brow, and Aine fell back against the pillow.

"Last year, this is all I wanted to do," I said.

"What's that?"

"Fall into bed with you instead of spending the next several hours on a flight back to the middle ages."

I'd had so many plans for us last Thanksgiving. We'd celebrated in Cambria like we were this year. I'd planned to whisk Aine away that night and drive up the coast to Big Sur where we'd spend a couple of nights at the Post Ranch Inn. Staying at the ultra-private resort would ensure that if we didn't want to see another human being, we wouldn't have had to. From there, I planned to take my time driving up the coast as far as Yachats, where I'd hoped we'd spend Christmas together.

This year, I hadn't even planned to see her, yet here we were, where it all began for us. So much had happened in the last three hundred and sixty-five days. I'd pushed her away and broken her heart.

What now, though? Everything I wanted to protect her from still lurked in the background.

"You're thinking too hard."

I smiled and looked down at her; she was studying me. "You're right. I am."

"What about?"

"Things I don't want to have on my mind, let alone talk about."

"The test?"

I nodded. "And more."

"Me?"

I kissed her forehead. "No matter what else is on my mind, you're there too. Twenty-four hours a day."

"Even when you sleep?"

"I dream about you every night."

"I dream of you too."

I knew, though, that wasn't the only thing that occupied her sleeping brain. The nightmares were there too. How could they not be? What worried me when we were together last year, was how seldom she talked about the ordeal she'd gone through when she and her friends were kidnapped and held captive for several days.

It had been a CIA-led investigation in conjunction with MI6 that had started the ball rolling on Aine's capture, and it had begun when Ava witnessed an incident with her ex-boyfriend that ultimately led both agencies to discover that the twin's father, Conor McNamara, was actually long-believed-dead arms dealer Makar Petrov.

Through the CIA, I'd arranged for protection for Ava, but not Aine, and that was something I regretted almost every day. If only I'd done things differently, had the forethought to realize she'd be in danger too, I could've spared her the horrific experience.

I groaned and looked up at the ceiling. Why did everything I regretted in life have to constantly play inside my head? It wasn't just my misguided thinking with the Petrov case. Everything I'd done that I wished I hadn't, ran a continual loop in my brain. Was that part of the disorder? Was it a symptom that would lead to a bipolar diagnosis?

"Stop," said Aine, rubbing my chest.

"Are you reading my mind?"

"It wouldn't be hard to do." Aine shifted so her arm was around me. "Griffin, I know you think you're doing what's best for me, but I'd liked to go to my sister's for Thanksgiving. I really want to see everyone."

Could I deny her anything when she looked at me like that? I smiled. "If that's what you want, that's what we'll do."

"Thank you," she murmured. "But before we go, I really need a shower."

40

Aine

Griffin had been so careful with me. He made sure my incision was completely covered, and then he showered with me. Each time I reached out to touch him, he teased that if I didn't stop, we'd be late for dinner.

There was no logical explanation for it, but when we drove through the gate of the beach house, I felt a sense of impending doom. Griffin picked up on it almost immediately.

"What's wrong?"

"I'm not sure. I just got a feeling."

"Do you want to go back to the inn?"

I shook my head. "No, I want to be here."

The feeling didn't go away when we walked inside.

"You were supposed to let me bring dinner to you," said Ava, meeting us at the door and glaring at Griffin.

"She insisted," he said, looking around the room. "Where is everybody?"

"If by 'everybody' you mean the boys, they're downstairs in the office."

"Okay if I join them?" he asked me.

"Don't worry. We'll take good care of her in your absence," Ava answered.

"Can I do anything to help?" I asked once Griffin was headed down the staircase.

"Yes. Go sit on the sofa and rest."

I rolled my eyes. "I can do something besides sit."

"I promised I'd take care of you. Now go, so Striker doesn't come back up and yell at me."

"Aine!" I heard Zary shout a few minutes later when she came through the front door with Lia in her arms. I tried to get up but had only gotten as far as putting my hands on either side of myself when Ava came out of the kitchen and pushed me back down.

Zary ran over and sat between the two of us, handing the baby to Ava and then gently hugging me.

"I'm so sorry I wasn't here," she said. "How are you?"

"I'm fine. Just sore." I looked over at baby Lia. "Can I hold her?"

Zary looked at Ava. "Would it be okay?"

Ava laughed. "Are you asking if I'll let her go or if it's okay if Aine holds her?"

Ava kissed Lia's cheek and handed her to Zary, who put her in my arms.

"She's so beautiful." I teared up, looking at my niece. She shared her mother's piercing blue eyes—identical to mine and Ava's. Her hair hadn't grown in much since the last time I'd seen her right after she was born, but what she had was light blonde, almost white, again like her mother's.

"Thank you," said Zary, gazing at her baby. "Tell me about your surgery."

Ava proceeded to tell our half sister what had happened down to the most minute detail, while I gazed at the baby.

"Is Sam sleeping?" I asked.

"No, he's next door with the grandmas and the girls."

I looked up when Pen and Tara came out of the kitchen with Merrigan.

"Our mom is the only one who isn't here," Ava said. "Gunner's and Zary's mothers, Madeline and Svetlana, are next door. So are Sally and Saylor, Tabon's mom and sister, along with Sierra and Savannah, his nieces."

"We met them at Christmas last year," said Pen.

"That's right. I completely forgot."

"I'm going to go check on the baby," said Merrigan. "Pen and Tara, you can come along if you'd like."

"No, thanks," Tara responded.

Penelope gave her a funny look and then shrugged. "I'll go."

A few seconds later, Tara walked out the front door.

"What is with her?" Ava asked, although I doubted she expected an answer.

41

Striker

"What's going on?" I asked Razor after saying hello to Doc, Gunner, and Mercer.

"I thought you weren't going to pull the trigger on Tackle and Halo deploying to Colombia," he responded.

"That's right. Yesterday I told you I wanted to wait and watch."

"Onyx's flight plan shows they left Miami two hours ago."

I was stunned. "What the hell?"

"You sure you didn't give Monk the green light?" Razor asked, rubbing his chin.

"You were here, Razor. I specifically said I wanted to keep everyone on standby for now. Monk confirmed it."

"Any chance he misunderstood?" asked Gunner.

My first inclination was to tear into him, but I held back. "None whatsoever," I answered, looking at Razor.

He nodded. "He's right. I was here. No way Striker and Monk got their signals crossed."

"Where is Monk?" asked Doc.

"No idea," I muttered.

"When's the last time you saw him?" Mercer asked.

As tense as I felt, Razor had to be feeling it too, considering the other three senior partners were grilling him as much as me.

"As Striker said, we met here yesterday afternoon. We talked about the fact that Ghafor was in Colombia, as well as the sudden movement of the weaponry. Also as Striker said, he was specific about not sending the team into Colombia."

"I talked to you too," said Doc, looking at me. "You were clear on standing down."

"We talked right after that," I said to Razor. "You asked whether we should stop the arms shipments, and I said not to. I asked you to tell Monk to keep his eyes on the shipments and on Ghafor. You told me then that you would when you saw him."

"That's right," said Razor.

"Where were you then?" asked Gunner.

"Right here in this fucking office," Razor growled back at him.

Doc held up his hand. "I don't think any one of us is questioning either Razor's or Striker's handling of this mission. I'd like us to be clear on that. What all of us are trying to get to the bottom of, is why Monk authorized a mission after Striker put the brakes on it."

"We're all making the assumption that he did," I said.

"You're right that we're making an assumption. However, it's based on the fact that he was assigned to be Tackle and Halo's handler, combined with the other fact that no one has seen him since yesterday," said Razor.

"What about your sister?" I asked him.

"I can check with her."

I nodded, and so did Doc.

"Where are Tackle and Halo now?" asked Gunner.

"Razor said, according to the flight plan, they left out of Miami two hours ago." Mercer was pulling something up on one of the monitors. "That would put them somewhere between Jamaica and Barranquilla."

I turned toward the door when I heard someone coming downstairs. I expected it to be Razor with an update on Monk from his sister. Instead, it was the man himself.

"Where in the hell have you been?" I was about to tear into him some more when I felt Doc's hand on my arm.

Monk looked at each of the men in the room, pushed past me, and sat in the chair next to Mercer.

"What's this?" he asked.

"Monk, I asked you a question. Where have you been?"

"Sleeping," he answered without turning around to look at me.

"Rhys."

Monk spun around and looked at Doc.

"Yáñez filed a flight plan earlier today," Doc said. "We aren't certain of the details, but it appears that he, Corazón, Tackle, and Halo are on their way to Colombia."

Monk glared at me. "I thought I was the handler on this."

"There he is," said Razor, coming back into the room, breathless.

"Anybody wanna tell me what the fuck is going on?" Monk asked.

Mercer stood, and I sat down in his place.

"Did you authorize their deployment?" I asked.

"Whose?"

"Jesus Christ, Monk! Tackle and Halo!" I was ready to pull my hair out.

"You said to put them on standby, and that's what I did."

I rubbed the back of my neck, trying my hardest not to rip into Monk more than I already was.

"Has anybody made contact with Yáñez?" he asked.

"Negative," Mercer answered.

"How'd you find out about the flight plan in the first place?" asked Gunner.

All eyes turned to Razor.

"I got a call from Jiménez, asking if Striker was on his way. I asked what he was talking about, and he responded that there was a K19 plane in the air."

"What did you tell him?" asked Doc.

"That his intel was bad," Razor answered.

"Meaning what exactly?"

"There was no K19 plane I knew of on its way to Colombia."

"What did he say?"

"He told me it was my intel that was bad."

"Has anyone actually confirmed the plane is even in the air?" asked Gunner.

Monk looked around the room, but everyone was looking at him. "I hadn't slept in forty-eight fucking hours," he muttered.

"Why didn't you tell anyone you were leaving?" Razor asked.

"Seriously?"

Razor stared him down.

"The last I checked, I was a partner in this fucking firm, and I don't ask permission." Monk stood to leave, but Doc put his hand on his arm.

"Monk, you're right. What we need to figure out now is whether there is a plane en route to Colombia. Once we've confirmed there is, we need to figure out who authorized its departure."

"I'll ask again, has anyone made contact with Yáñez?"

"Negative, Monk," answered Razor like Mercer had in his absence. "I've attempted contact with all four we believe are on board—Onyx, Corazón, Tackle, and Halo. No response."

"You *believe* to be on board? Have you seen the flight plan? What about the manifest?" Monk was angrier than I ever remembered seeing him.

"Negative. There hasn't been time," Razor answered.

"How long since you spoke to Jiménez?" I asked Razor, who checked his phone.

"Thirteen-ten."

"It's thirteen-thirty-five now. My answer, Monk, is we've been trying to figure this out in real time. We need your help."

Monk nodded, picking up his phone.

"Gentlemen," said Razor, motioning for everyone to leave the room. "I can't believe I'm saying this, but we have several women upstairs who have been cooking for the last few days in order to serve a large group of people Thanksgiving dinner."

"Understood. We'll eat in shifts," answered Doc.

"That'll work," said Razor. "I'll let them know."

Doc turned to me. "How's Aine?"

"Stable. I doubt anyone is letting her lift a finger."

"I'll head up and speak with Merrigan. Striker, who do you want to stay down here with you and Monk?"

"I'll stay." Mercer volunteered before I could answer. It would've been whom I would've asked for anyway.

"Gunner, let's go."

Before he followed Doc, he turned around and got in my face. "You find out anything, you need anything, you say so immediately."

I nodded. "Copy that, and thank you."

Gunner grunted something I didn't hear.

"Fuck," I heard Monk say beneath his breath.

I sat down beside him. "What?"

"It's all here. Flight plan, manifest, departure log."

"Out of Miami?"

"Atlanta."

I was about to ask why, but did it matter? The four had been on the East Coast and on standby. We'd never asked for anyone's twenty. We just assumed that Monk would orchestrate this part of the mission when and if he was given the go-ahead.

"Where are they now?" I asked.

"That's the thing," Monk said, shaking his head. "They're nowhere."

"Come again?"

Monk pointed first to one monitor and then the other. "That's the last flight segment before they went silent. This is a hundred-mile radius." He motioned with his head to the other two monitors. "These are five hundred and one thousand miles."

I could see the flight path clearly, but shortly after thirteen hundred hours, the plane, which had just crossed into Venezuela near Punta Fijo, seemed to vanish into thin air. I knew the aircraft well, along with the technology onboard—Air Force One had a better chance of disappearing than it had.

"Have you made contact with Venezuelan air traffic?" I asked.

"I'm doing that now," Mercer answered.

I pinged Razor with an SOS. Seconds later, he was back downstairs.

"Get everyone back down here," I told him.

"Roger that," he said, turning around.

By the time Mercer hung up, all eyes were on him. "The power grid is completely shut down."

"What do you mean?" asked Gunner.

"The entire country is dark."

"That's impossible."

Monk was listening to something through the headset. "It's not. President Maduro just announced a state of emergency. Get the feed," he said to me.

"Here it is." I turned the monitor's volume up. "Emergency radio," I explained when nothing appeared on the screen.

We listened as the country's current president accused José Guaidós, the US-backed incoming leader of Venezuela, of sabotaging the power grid.

"They have one fucking grid," muttered Gunner, shaking his head.

I listened to the rest of the broadcast, jotting down key phrases. Everyone in the room spoke Spanish, among other languages, but I understood what Maduro was saying between the lines better than the others did. If there were a part of the world more fucked up than the Middle East right now, Venezuela would be at the top of the list.

Razor rubbed the back of his neck. "It doesn't explain why we lost contact, or why the plane isn't showing up on the radar. Neither would be affected by one country's grid."

"It would if they were diverting and/or blocking signals," Monk responded.

"What about Jiménez?" Doc asked.

"My gut is telling me to leave him out of this."

Doc nodded.

"Anything?" I asked. Monk shook his head. I studied the same monitors he was, hoping the plane would miraculously reappear.

Five minutes later, Razor's voice cut through the quiet of the room. "Is anyone thinking the same thing I am?"

Doc rubbed the back of his neck with his hand like Razor had. "Four of our teammates are on a plane that was last seen in Venezuelan airspace. We know their government isn't going to do a damn thing to help us find it. We can't do this alone. We need to contact the agency."

"I'm not on the best of terms with McTiernan over the Ghafor clusterfuck," I warned.

"I'll engage Cope instead," Doc offered.

While Sumner Copeland worked for the man I was at odds with, the fact that K19 had expressed an interest in extending him an offer of employment made him a logical go-between.

I looked at Razor, who nodded.

"If we think this plane is down, I'm going in."

"I'm with you, Striker," said Razor. "Who else?"

Every hand went up.

"Happy fucking Thanksgiving," grumbled Gunner.

"You're not—"

When Gunner shot me a look, I shut up.

"You don't know anything if you think I'd sit here on my ass." He walked out of the room, shaking his head. "Who put him in charge?" we heard him mutter.

"I did," both Doc and Razor answered when Gunner pushed past them.

I sat down next to Monk. "You tell me. What should we do?"

"Best if we split into teams. One to Bogotá and one closer to where the plane lost contact," he answered.

"Flying into Maracaibo would make the most sense, but would it even be possible with Venezuela's power grid down?"

Monk shook his head. "The closest we can get is Aruba."

"Cope can arrange for aircraft and pilots," said Doc.

Monk pointed to the screen at what looked like a radar report. "No one is going anywhere until tomorrow at the earliest."

While it was late in the season and both Aruba and Colombia were below the hurricane belt, in order to get to either, we'd have to fly directly through the eye of an impending storm.

Not only would it ground us, it would make any search for the aircraft and its occupants exponentially more difficult.

"It's Cope again," said Doc, looking at his phone. He walked into the hallway to take the call.

"Where's the fucking plane?" I muttered.

"Tabon?" I heard Ava call out from the stairwell.

"Monk, is there anything else we can do right now?"

He shook his head.

"Go eat, then."

Monk didn't acknowledge that Razor had said anything.

"He means you."

Monk turned and looked into my eyes. "I need quiet to do this."

I nodded and motioned for everyone to head out.

"I'll be back in a few minutes."

"I'll let you know if I need you."

"Not a word about this," Doc unnecessarily warned everyone in the room.

I followed the group upstairs.

When I reached the top, I saw Aine seated on the sofa. Her back was to me, yet I could still feel the anxiety emanating from her. I understood and agreed with Doc's mandate not to discuss the missing plane; however, I had to tell her something or she'd be eaten up with worry. My guess was Ava, Quinn, and Zary would feel the same way. Merrigan had likely already been read in.

I came around to where Aine sat and held my hand out to her. "I hear it's time to eat."

"Something is going on that you can't tell me about."

Aine didn't phrase it as a question, but I sat down and answered her anyway. "That's right."

We'd talked about it more than once, earlier this year, when we were still together. She had enough experience to know my limits without me being specific. She could read me, though, like she had now.

"Do you have to leave?" she asked.

"Not yet."

"But soon?"

I nodded and pulled her close. I'd already told her I might have to return to Colombia, although now the reason was entirely different.

"I wish we'd stayed at the inn."

"We can go back now if you'd like."

Aine shook her head. "After dinner."

"Does anyone know where Tara is?" Pen asked, coming in from next door.

"She walked out right after you did," said Ava.

"Wait a minute." Pen walked into the kitchen. "I can't believe this." She came back out with her hands on her hips.

"What?" Aine asked.

"She took the car."

"I'm sure she'll be back soon. She knows what time we're having dinner," said Quinn.

"Which is now," added Ava when Razor shouted that he was finished carving the turkey. "It isn't as though we're all sitting down at one big table. She can eat when she gets back."

I watched the exchange and then walked over to Penelope, who looked more distressed than the rest of them. "Are you okay?"

"She took the car."

"I heard."

"The rental agreement is in my name."

"This is probably a stupid question, but have you called her?"

Pen nodded a second time. "She didn't answer."

"Try the rental company."

"Why?"

"Some of them track the cars. I can do it for you if you'd like?"

Pen looked across the room to where Aine was seated on the sofa. "I can do it, but thank you."

"Let me know what you find out."

I stayed by Aine's side, insisting that I make her a plate from the Thanksgiving buffet her sister had commandeered, and then return it to the kitchen when she finished eating.

There were conversations all around us from the crowd of people gathered for the holiday meal. Aine and I managed to stay on the perimeter of the chaos, not talking, but not needing to, as though our bodies and minds were so in tune that we communicated silently.

Once we finished our pie, Aine asked if we could leave.

"I need to talk to Doc and Razor..."

She nodded. "I'll track down Ava."

"I'll find her and send her to you."

"I can walk, Griffin."

I knelt down and kissed her. "You are dead-on-your-tush tired, sweetheart. Let your sister come to you."

"Okay," she murmured, as though even speaking the word took energy she didn't have.

Before I went in search of Razor and Ava, I found Penelope out on the deck.

"Any luck?" I asked.

"No. That agency doesn't have GPS on their cars."

I didn't tell her this, but given the ordeal that the four women had gone through over a year ago, it was likely K19 still had tracking installed on Tara's phone.

"Aine wants to go back to the inn, but let Razor know if you need him to jump in on this."

"Like Ava said earlier, she'll be back when she's back."

I went inside and found Razor in the kitchen with his wife and son. "Aine's ready to go."

Razor nodded, handing Sam to his wife.

"Why don't you just stay here?" Ava suggested. "It'll be more comfortable for her."

It would solve the current dilemma of not wanting to leave Aine alone, but also needing to be here.

"We'll go to the inn instead," said Zary, looking at Gunner.

"Hold off anyone going anywhere," said Razor. "We can figure this out."

"What about Butler Ranch?" Quinn said to Doc, who had walked in with Merrigan.

"I'm headed there now," Merrigan responded.

"I'm sure they have plenty of room since only one of my brothers still lives there," said Doc.

"You aren't going with Merrigan?" Quinn asked.

Mercer leaned forward and whispered something in her ear that I couldn't hear. Quinn nodded.

"It's going to be a late night, then," she said, looking at Ava, who nodded.

"I'll host a girls' night at our place," Quinn offered. "It'll be a little rustic, though."

"We could all go to Butler Ranch," suggested Merrigan.

I excused myself. I didn't care who went where as long as I didn't have to leave Aine alone.

"Got a minute?" I asked Razor, who followed me out of the crowded kitchen.

"What's up?"

"Can we still track the girls' phones?"

"By girls, do you mean Ava's group of friends?"

I nodded.

"Affirmative."

"Penelope is pretty concerned about Tara."

"Say no more. I'll get on it."

An hour later, I knew I should go back downstairs. But with Aine asleep next to me in the king-size bed, I didn't want to.

When I heard the front door open, though, I shot out of bed and went to see who had come in.

"How's she doing?" whispered Razor.

"Asleep for now. Any news?"

"We got a ping from the plane."

"Where is it?"

"Coordinates indicate Macuira National Park. There's a team headed there now, but with the storm, I don't know if they'll be able to reach it."

I didn't want to say out loud what both of us knew this meant.

"I don't know if you're a praying man, but if you are, now's the time to ask God to watch over our crew," Razor said before walking back out the front door.

42

Aine

I turned around and went back to the bedroom, but too late. I'd already heard what Griffin wouldn't have wanted me to. I couldn't lie or hide it from him, though.

"I heard you and Tabon talking," I said when he joined me in the bedroom.

"I was going to tell you anyway, as soon as we knew anything." He cupped my cheek with his hand. "It appears the K19 plane went down in a forested area in the northern part of Colombia."

"Who was on it?"

"Onyx, Corazón, Tackle, and Halo."

I'd heard all those names before and had met everyone but Corazón.

When Griffin crawled into bed next to me, I slid back under the covers, wrapped my arm around his waist, and rested my head on his chest.

"It could have been me on that plane. Maybe it should've been," he said a few minutes later.

"Why do you say you should have been?"

"It was my mission they were carrying out."

"But you weren't on it, because you were with me."

I felt him nod. Was he thankful, or did he regret he hadn't been there in place of one of the others?

"If it went down, it's unlikely there are survivors."

"I know."

He tightened his arms around me. "Am I hurting you?" he asked, pulling back.

"Not at all."

He was quiet for several minutes. When he did speak, he asked me to look at him.

"We have so much unfinished between us," he murmured. "I love you. You know that?"

"I love you too, Griffin."

"I've been doing a lot of thinking."

"What about?"

"The test."

I reached up and kissed his cheek. "Whatever you want to do, I'll support."

"I'm going to do it."

"I will too."

Regardless of the combined outcomes, chances were that one or both of us would be unable to have children—him by choice, and me by my inability to get pregnant.

"What's involved?" I asked.

"I have the kit with me. I've had it for weeks."

"Do you have to go to a hospital?"

"No. I just swab the inside of my cheek, put it in the container, and drop it in the mail. Can you believe something so simple could irrevocably change my life?"

"Both our lives." I rested my head back on his chest. "How long before you get the results?"

"Three to five weeks."

"I have to wait six weeks before I can even take the test to see if my remaining ovary is functioning."

"How long for the results?"

"I don't know."

Griffin kissed my forehead and then both sides of my face, my eyelids, and then my lips. When a tear ran down my cheek, he kissed it away.

"We'll wait and find out the results of both together."

"Okay," I whispered.

"And, Aine?"

"Yeah?"

"Whatever the outcome, we face it together too."

I smiled at his use of the words I'd said to him at the hospital. "That's all that matters to me, Griffin. That we're together."

"There's something else I want you to do for me. It's something I've given a lot of thought to."

"Okay."

"I want you to research bipolar disorder as well as schizophrenia. Not for me. I want you to have a clear understanding so if we decide to make a go of this relationship, you know what kind of baggage I might be bringing along."

I nodded again, understanding what he was asking me to do and why. If our situations were reversed, I'd like to think I'd suggest the same thing.

"I may do further research, if that's okay with you."

"Of course it is. What kind?"

"Gene therapy. I won't get into it now, but great strides are being made in that area with genetic mutations and variations."

Griffin smiled.

"What?"

"Do you know how proud I am of you?"

"Me?" I felt my cheeks heat, and I looked away.

Griffin put his finger on my chin and turned my head back toward him. "That's all on me."

"What is?"

"You doubting yourself. I can't tell you how much I regret making you feel like you weren't enough."

I didn't know what to say. In my mind, I still wasn't, no matter what he said now. Griffin had so many more life experiences than me.

"Remember earlier when you told me to stop thinking so hard about whatever it was that I had on my mind?" he asked.

"Yes. You're telling me to do the same thing."

"I'm telling you to sleep."

"I am pretty tired." I snuggled into him and closed my eyes.

"Will you be okay on your own if I go next door for a few minutes?"

"Yes, dear."

43

Striker

One side of my heart was smiling solely because of Aine, but the other was full of regret. Getting a ping from the aircraft without communication from its pilot or anyone else on board meant they were likely dead.

This was my mission, and everything that took place in the course of it was ultimately my responsibility. It had been my decision initially to send Tackle and Halo into Colombia, regardless of whether I pulled the trigger on it or not.

Who had was as big a mystery as I'd ever had to solve. It was obvious by Monk's reaction that it wasn't him. And since he hadn't either, who in the hell had? Who would Onyx have listened to if it wasn't me or one of the other K19 partners?

None of it made any sense.

"DEA have the coordinates of the plane. No one has gotten close yet due to the storm combined with the terrain," Razor reported when I walked into the office.

I turned to Doc. "How soon can Cope arrange transport?"

"Do we know if we can even fly yet? What's the status of the hurricane?" Razor asked.

"Planes and crew are on standby at LAX. I've been told they're cleared to fly."

"Can we get transport arranged from here to there?" I asked. It was a five-hour drive from Cambria to Los Angeles. We couldn't afford that kind of time followed by a seven-plus hour flight.

"Affirmative," said Mercer. "There's a CH-53K out of Vandenberg that can get us there in under an hour."

"Let's move." I didn't know who intended to follow me, but it didn't matter. I was going in, even if it was alone.

Doc motioned to a door I hadn't paid attention to. "Get as much of your gear together as you can from here."

"What's in there?"

"Full tactical gear, plus what's in the safe. I'll give Merrigan an inventory of whatever else we need while we're on the road to the airfield. She'll make arrangements to have it delivered to the plane in Los Angeles."

"You mean planes, right, Doc?" asked Gunner.

"Affirmative. We'll split into two groups. Striker, who do you want with you?"

"Me," said Razor.

"And me," said Monk.

Doc waited for my response.

"That's the first team," I said. Before I could ask if Mercer was in, I saw the man coming out of the small storage area with his arms full.

"Gunner, Mercer, and I will be team two."

"What about Ranger and Diesel?" Razor asked me. I looked at Doc.

"Let me see what Cope can do. What's their twenty?"

"Right outside DC."

"Shouldn't be too difficult, then. Striker?"

"We'll head out in fifteen?"

As much as I didn't want to wake Aine, there was no way I could leave without saying goodbye.

When I walked in the front door, she was walking toward me.

"I wasn't sure you'd be awake."

"You have to leave, don't you?"

"I do, sweetheart." I kissed her. "I wish I didn't have to," I whispered. "It's wrecking me inside."

"I know," she whispered too. "You have no choice, Griffin. I know you don't."

I looked at my watch and kissed her again, this time more deeply.

"I have to go. I'll be in touch as much as I can, as soon as I can. If you have any questions, ask Merrigan. I love you, Aine."

"I love you, Griffin." She tightened her arms around my neck. "Please stay safe. Please come back to me," she said into my ear, her eyes filling with tears.

Instead of leaving, I led her over to the sofa and pulled her onto my lap.

"What are you doing? You need to leave."

"I can stay a couple more minutes."

I wiped her tears and kissed her again.

"I'm scared," she whispered.

"I wish I could promise you that nothing will happen to me or anyone else on our team, but you know as well as I do that isn't a promise I can make."

"I do know that."

"Our conversation probably isn't much different than others taking place right now." I sighed. "I'm sorry. I've got to go."

"Do you have your compass?"

I smiled and pulled it from my pocket. "I never go anywhere without it." I kissed her one last time. "I love you."

44

Aine

I followed Striker out the door and stood on the front step with Zary, Quinn, Merrigan, and Saylor. When I turned to go inside, I saw that Gunner's mother and Razor's mother were behind us.

"It's never easy," said Merrigan, putting her arm around my shoulders. "If I told you it gets more so, I'd be lying."

When I walked inside, Ava was standing with Sam in her arms.

"Auntie Aine needs a big hug, Sam." My sister motioned me toward the sofa, and when I sat down, she lowered Sam onto my lap. "Is this okay?" she asked.

"It's perfect."

"He isn't hurting you, right?"

I rested my head against the baby's. "No, he's taking the hurt away."

A few minutes later, Penelope walked inside from the deck, looking at her phone.

"I swear I'm going to kill her," she mumbled.

"Tara?" asked Ava.

Pen nodded.

"What's going on with you two?" I asked.

"It isn't us two; it's just her."

Penelope dropped into a chair and threw her phone on the table. "I'm getting so tired of her bullshit."

"Talk," said Ava, sitting down next to me and Sam on the sofa.

"I should've known something was up when I had to buy her ticket."

Ava leaned forward. "What are you talking about?"

"It didn't seem like a big deal at the time, but she had a problem with her credit card when she tried to buy it."

"Are you talking about Tara?" asked Quinn, coming in and flopping down on another chair.

"She's bitchier than usual," said Pen.

Quinn nodded. "I don't think she's more of one than all of us have been at some point in our lives."

Penelope shook her head. "No, it's worse. A lot worse. Today she took off with the car, and I have no idea where she is. Remember the credit card issue? Guess whose name the rental is in."

"Hmm," said Quinn, looking at her phone.

"*What?*" all three of us asked.

"Are you aware that Tara's father is being investigated for wire fraud?"

"No," gasped Ava. "What does it say?"

Quinn read the short article she found online out loud.

"I guess that explains the credit card issue."

"Maybe she's just embarrassed," said Quinn.

"Of what?" Ava stood and walked over to the sliding glass door. "Her father's being investigated for wire fraud. Our father tried to *kill* us."

"Have you called her?" I asked Pen.

"Just once every fifteen minutes. She won't answer her phone."

Ava stood and walked over to the window. "She's pulling in now."

"*Where in the hell have you been?*" Pen shouted when Tara walked in the front door.

"*What the fuck?*" Tara shouted back, making me cringe.

"You just take off without a word to anyone. You wouldn't answer your phone. We were worried about you."

Tara laughed. "Right. How long did it take before you even noticed I wasn't here?"

"Look," Pen said, lowering her voice. "We know about your dad."

"What about him?"

"Don't play stupid. The investigation."

"I don't know what you're talking about."

I tried to make eye contact with Pen. Tara wasn't lying. This was news to her.

"Come sit," I said, motioning to her.

"I have to call my dad," Tara answered, rushing out to the deck and closing the sliding door behind her.

Pen walked over and sat beside me. "I'm really worried about her."

"I am too."

"I think she might be..."

"What? It's just us here," said Ava. "She might be what?"

"It's almost like she's on something."

Tara came back inside, wiping the tears from her face. "I hope you're all happy now. Thanks for blindsiding me."

"Wait a minute," said Pen, standing. "No one blindsided you, and why would any of us be happy that your father is being investigated?"

"I need to go back to New York," she announced as though Pen hadn't said a word.

"So go." Pen sat back down.

"Come with me," said Quinn, pulling Tara by the hand.

"How much do you want to bet that Quinn is buying her a ticket?" said Pen, crossing her arms.

"What would be wrong with that?" I asked.

"Nothing," she muttered. "But I'm done."

"Being her friend? You don't mean that. She needs us now more than ever."

Pen rested her chin in her hand. "You're right, as much as I don't want to admit it."

I looked up at my sister, who was digging in her purse. "You're being awfully quiet."

"I'll be right back..." Her words trailed off as she walked out of the room.

"What was that all about?" asked Pen.

"No clue. Is it just me, or is there weirdness all around us?"

"It isn't you."

"I'm giving Tara a ride to the airport," Quinn said when she came back in the room with Tara trailing behind her.

"Bye," said Tara, waving.

"Wait," Pen called out to her as she was walking out the front door. "How about a hug? And what about Aine?"

Tara walked over as though what Pen had asked her to do was the worst thing she could imagine. She gave us both perfunctory hugs and walked back toward the door where Quinn waited.

"What about Ava?" I asked.

"Tell her I said thank you."

Without another word, Tara walked out; Quinn shrugged her shoulders and followed.

I closed my eyes, saying a silent prayer, like I did at least once every half hour, that God would keep Griffin and the rest of the K19 team safe, but this time, I included Tara.

"Where is she?" shouted Ava.

"Who? Pen?" I asked.

"I don't care where Pen is. Where's Tara?"

"She left with Quinn to go to the airport. What's wrong?"

"When did they leave?"

"*Ava*! Sit down and tell me what's wrong."

When she came closer, I could see that Ava had her wallet in her hand.

"She cleaned me out," said Ava.

"What are you talking about?"

"My cash is gone. Where's your wallet?"

"I don't even know where my bag is. Griffin carried it in for me."

"I'll look," said Ava, standing back up. "Where's Penelope?"

"I don't know that either. I must've fallen asleep."

I watched as Ava looked around the room, then went into the kitchen. She came back out and opened the front hall closet.

"Here it is," she said, bringing it over to me. "How much cash did you have?" she asked.

"I don't know. Not much, if any."

I slowly opened the change compartment. I had a habit when I was traveling; I'd put whatever small jewelry I was wearing in that part of my wallet so I wouldn't accidentally leave it behind. When I saw it was empty, my eyes filled with tears.

"What's missing?" asked Ava, sitting down and putting a hand on my arm.

"The bracelet Griffin gave me for Christmas. The one that belonged to his aunt."

The front door opened, and Pen walked in. "What's wrong?" she asked, looking into my tear-filled eyes.

"We're missing some money and some other things," Ava said. "How long ago did Tara leave?"

Pen looked at her phone. "I don't know, maybe thirty minutes."

Ava was already making a call. "Quinn, where's Tara?"

I was sitting close enough that I could hear Quinn say that our friend was already on the plane and she was on her way back from the airport.

"What did she say?" Pen asked after Ava hung up.

"Tara's flying to LAX and getting a connecting flight to New York from there. Quinn is on her way back now." Ava clenched her fists. "I'm so mad," she muttered.

"We don't know it was Tara."

Both Ava and Pen looked at me like I'd gone crazy.

"Who else would it have been?" asked Ava.

"I don't know. All I'm saying is that we don't know it was Tara."

I turned my head when my eyes filled with tears, thinking about my lost bracelet. Griffin had entrusted me with something priceless, and now it was missing. If only I hadn't taken it off before we took a shower at the inn.

I thought back to the feeling of foreboding I had when we arrived here, hoping beyond hope that nothing else went wrong.

45

Striker

"I want to run something by you," said Razor once we were on the plane that would take us to Colombia.

"Shoot."

"I have an idea what Ghafor is stockpiling weapons for, or who—FARC."

I nodded. It wasn't a surprise to hear Razor's theory, given the tentative peace agreement the Marquez-led Colombian government and the Revolutionary Armed Forces of Colombia, aka FARC, came to a few short years ago was already falling apart.

I'd expected it wouldn't be long before it did after the last Colombian election. The then-president and broker of the peace, Francisco Marquez, was defeated by Petro Santos, who had emerged the leader of those opposed to the treaty.

I was on the team that had negotiated the surrender of over eight thousand weapons from a number of FARC combatants reported to be twice that.

The treaty had been historic in that it had taken fifty years to bring the conflict to an end, but the implementation of the accord was beyond optimistic. The government and FARC weren't the only two entities vying for power in Colombia—the drug cartels had more power than each of the two on their own, but less if they joined forces.

No matter who was involved—politicians, insurgents, or drug barons—corruption was rampant. Not to mention the Islamic fundamentalists who had settled in Buenaventura. The entire country was a ticking time bomb.

"At least we know what we're dealing with when it comes to FARC, the government, and even the cartels. For me, the big unknown is the Islamics," said Razor.

"What's your take on Jiménez?" I asked.

"Don't trust him," Monk muttered.

I raised my head. I hadn't realized he was paying attention, although why wouldn't he be?

"Yeah, Monk?" said Razor. "What's your take?"

Monk was a hard man to read, but his combined anger and pain sat too close to the surface for anyone to miss. "Think about it," he spat. "Jiménez agrees to meet with Striker; Juan Carlos is killed between the time you leave the States and arrive in Colombia; Ghafor moves the arms, and the peace treaty falls apart."

"Who do you think is orchestrating this?"

I paid more attention to Monk's physical responses to Razor's questions than to his answers.

"One of the cartels makes the most sense," I said.

Monk nodded. "Keep going."

"Which one has Jiménez in their pocket?" asked Razor.

"All of them."

I agreed.

"There are no good guys," Monk muttered.

He was right. Whatever was happening in Colombia, the US had to go on the assumption that there was no one they could trust, from the president down.

"We should let 'em annihilate each other."

"If only." I shook my head. "What about the plane? You think this is a coincidence, Monk?"

"Fuck no. Somebody set us up."

"Any idea who?"

"How'd you find out the plane was in the air?"

"Jiménez contacted me."

"Exactly. Here's my question—how the hell did anyone know that I was the handler on the op? Someone like Jiménez could've assumed you were the lead, but why would Onyx pull the trigger on the flight plan without checking in with me first?"

"You didn't hear a word from him?"

"You don't think that's the first place I went? Not a fucking word."

"I heard you were on board," said a man I hadn't seen in years. "How the heck are you, Ellis?"

I shook his hand. "Good to see you, Trap. Still with the agency, huh?"

"Yep, and drivin' the bus. I've got an ex-wife and two daughters that I'll eventually have to put through college, man."

"Ouch," I said, pointing to my teammates. "You know Razor Sharp and Monk Perrin. Boys, this is Trap Flannery. We go way back to my first day at the agency."

"We haven't met although I've heard of both of you."

Monk didn't appear to have heard a word the man said; however, that was more his MO than all the talking he'd done in the last few minutes.

"Hey, I heard Butler snagged Fatale."

"Don't ever let her hear you say something like that, Trap."

"Who's flying with you?" Razor asked him.

"Someone you know pretty well." Trap pointed at the bridge. "Here he is now."

"Hello, boys," said Mantis Gehring as he walked on the plane, followed by someone else we knew pretty well—Dutch Miller.

"Heard some of ours are MIA," said Dutch, putting his hand on my shoulder. "Can't believe you didn't call me."

"Heard you were retired."

Dutch patted his stomach. "Retired? Shit. I'm in the best shape of my life."

"Thanks to Malin," said Mantis, giving Dutch a shove.

"I'm happy to give my bride all the credit in the world, for pretty much everything."

"Good to see you two," I said, shaking both their hands. "Even though the circumstances suck. How's your wife?"

"Alegria's doing the full-time-mom thing."

"Congratulations on the little tyke," said Razor.

"Thanks. He's a couple of weeks old, and yet he rules our roost. Have you heard Dutch is gonna be a dad too?"

"Wow. How is Malin?"

The woman had been the driving force behind the arrest and conviction of several high-ranking CIA agents and governmental officials. We could use someone with her brain on this mission, and I told Dutch so.

"I don't know if she'll ever be ready to return to the workforce, and I support her one hundred percent on that decision. For now, her full-time job is incubation."

Razor clapped Dutch on the back. "Congratulations to you too," he said. "When's she due?"

"April of next year."

"Happy for you, man," I said, shaking Dutch's hand.

"What about you? When are you gonna add to our future workforce?"

I forced a smile; Dutch had no idea how painful that question would be for me to answer.

46

Striker

The minute the plane landed, Razor's, Monk's and my phone blew up. I read the texts first before listening to the messages, but each one was from someone asking me to check in as soon as I landed.

I tried Doc first, but the call went straight to voicemail, so I called Cope.

"What's happening?" I asked when he answered.

"Did you listen to your messages?"

"No."

"DEA agents found the plane."

"And?"

Razor's and Monk's heads shot up at my raised voice.

"I'm waiting for confirmation as to the specifics, but the word I received was there were three critically injured and one fatality."

I put my head in my hands and turned toward the window. "*Goddammit.* Where are they?"

"As you know, the plane was found in Macuira National Park. Because of the situation in Venezuela, the survivors were airlifted to the university hospital in

Magdalena. I've made arrangements for a private aircraft to take you to Simón Bolívar International Airport where a car will take you directly to the hospital."

"Who's the fatality, Cope?" I asked, making eye contact with Razor and Monk, who both hung their heads.

"I'm sorry, Striker. I don't have confirmation on that yet."

"Who knows about this?"

"Which part?"

"The next leg of our trip."

"Right now, you, me, the owner of the plane, Mantis, and Trap. He'll make the rest of the arrangements as soon as you've deboarded."

"Tell me, Cope, do the DEA agents think the crash was accidental?"

"Not sure yet, but there's a crew headed to the wreckage to investigate."

"Where's the black box?"

"With the DEA until the investigators arrive."

"How soon until we head out?"

"Like I said, Trap is making the arrangements."

"What about the rest of our team?"

"Working on transport for Doc, Gunner, and Eighty-eight now."

"Ranger and Diesel?"

"In the air. We'll make that determination after you arrive at the hospital."

"Thanks, Cope. If you hear anything about the condition of our people, contact me immediately."

"Roger that, and, Striker, Godspeed."

"Hey, wait. Who's the plane's owner?"

Cope hesitated, which sent my blood pressure up. "I can't tell you that, but I need you to trust me."

"*Fuck*," I muttered, hating that for now, I had to accept not knowing. If Cope's boss had said the same thing, I would've had a hard time doing as he asked. I prayed that I was putting my trust into one of the good guys.

Before we deboarded, I briefed Razor and Monk on what I'd learned.

"He wouldn't tell you whose plane we're flying out on?" Razor asked.

"That's right." I looked up when Trap came out of the cockpit. Before I realized what was happening, Monk had the man by the neck.

"*Whose plane is it? Tell me right fucking now.*"

Trap's eyes met mine, and I nodded.

"Franz Lehrer's."

Monk released Trap and shoved him away.

"We're taking a fucking Armenian-born drug baron's plane? In what universe would anyone agree to this?"

Trap rubbed the back of his neck. "The one where the CIA is working with him to take down the Cali Cartel, FARC, and Petro Santos."

"Jesus Christ." I shook my head, taking in the weighted words of what Trap had just said.

The theory Razor and I had come up with before the flight, of the treaty between the FARC combatants and the Colombian government falling apart, couldn't have been more off base.

Instead, they were working together, along with Mao's Cali Cartel, to ensure an end to Latin America's oldest and most stable democracy.

"What about Ghafor and the weapons?"

"Buenaventura is in Medellín-controlled territory."

"Ghafor's working with the CIA."

"You didn't really think we were that stupid, did you, Striker?" said Trap.

"Not all of you."

"Don't underestimate McTiernan," Trap added. "You didn't suspect a thing."

"Who supplied the weapons?"

We all looked at Monk.

"United fucking Russia," he answered.

It made perfect sense. I should've known the CIA wouldn't let someone like Ghafor choose his place of exile. They put him where they wanted him and gave him a very specific mission—to help them get rid of Santos, put Marquez back in power, and save the crumbling democracy before it was too late.

The money, wherever it really came from, flowed through the Medellín cartel, to the Islamic State, to UR, who then supplied the weapons—believing the endgame was to reinforce Santos' power.

Instead, Ghafor made arrangements to have the arms shipped to Colombia in order to fuel the bloodbath I'd predicted would take place. The one in which Franz's cartel would reign victorious over Mao's. More importantly though, Franz and the Islamic State would have the combined ability to take down the Santos administration as well as FARC—all thanks to the United States of America.

If word of this got out, that the CIA corroborated with one of the largest drug cartels in Colombia, it might bring the agency itself down. The US had recently lost one president due to one of the biggest conspiracies in the nation's history. The one I found myself in the middle of was almost as big.

"How high up does this go, Trap?"

"I can't answer that."

My level of anger rose to the equivalent of Monk's. "Three of our team are critically injured. One is dead. I want to know who's responsible."

Trap shook his head. "I'm sorry, Striker."

"Why was our plane in the air in the first place? No one from K19 authorized Onyx's flight plan. No one pulled the trigger on that part of the mission. I want to know who did, when, and why."

When Trap shook his head again, I pushed past him and got off the plane, hoping Razor would keep Monk from ripping into the pilot. The only way I could stop myself from doing the same thing was to put as much distance as I could between me and the man who knew the answers to my questions but was refusing to share them.

As I paced inside the private area of the terminal, questions repeated in my head.

Why would the CIA want K19 in Colombia? Particularly since the men in question had only recently left the agency. Someone on the plane was working for the opposition. That was the only logical answer. Or someone on the K19 team that stayed on the ground was. Who, though? As I ran through the list of partners and employees, no one made sense.

When I raised my head, Trap was standing just inside the doorway.

"Whose side were they on?"

"The wrong one."

"Who shot down the fucking plane?"

"Not our side."

"Tell me, Trap, whose side am I on?"

"Ours."

"Who was it? Tell me *right fucking now.*"

"Corazón."

"Who was she working for?"

"Santos."

I sat down and put my head in my hands. "Why did Jiménez call Razor to confirm I was on that plane?"

"Corazón wanted him to believe you were in order to arrange a meeting between the ambassador, Lehrer, and Ghafor. He was on our side."

"What about the mole? Who knew I was on my way to Colombia? Who killed Juan Carlos?"

"I can't answer that."

"Meaning the agency was behind it. There never was a fucking mole."

Trap didn't respond.

"Corazón wanted Jiménezo believe I was on my way so she could arrange to have all the players in the same room at the same time."

"That's right."

"She's an assassin."

Trap nodded. "She was."

"She was the fatality."

"Affirmative."

"Piece it together for me."

"We believe she was able to convince Onyx that they had the go-ahead to deploy."

Of course Onyx hadn't questioned her; they were in a relationship.

"Once they were in the air, Corazón intercepted the messages coming in from your team. K19 wasn't the only one trying to reach Onyx to divert. We were too."

"And in the midst of it, the plane went down."

Trap looked out the window. "It's all hypothetical, Striker."

I pictured the scene in my head. Onyx must've somehow figured out Corazón was intercepting the messages and then knew she'd lied to him. Maybe he even realized she was working for the other side. My guess was that once Corazón realized Onyx was onto her, she tried to kill him. Or vice versa. We wouldn't know the whole story until Onyx was able to tell it.

As my conversation with Trap transpired, one by one, the K19 team members who had been on the plane, filed into the terminal's waiting area.

"I'm having a hard time wrapping my head around this," said Dutch. "Corazón and Onyx were tight."

I looked out on the tarmac; another plane was taxiing in.

Trap saw it too. "The rest of your team has arrived."

I waited for Doc, Gunner, and Mercer to come inside before briefing them on what I'd learned from Trap about the downed aircraft.

"A minute?" Trap asked. I followed him out of the waiting room and back out onto the tarmac. "As I'm sure you can understand, I cannot brief your entire team on the rest of what I told you earlier."

"I can."

"I'm officially telling you not to."

"I don't give a shit."

"I'll ask this, then. Keep it to as much of a minimum as you can until this finishes playing out."

"Are you asking me to sit on my hands while a civil war wages in this country?"

"I am."

"I need to get my people the fuck out of here."

"That's the plan."

"We need to read Doc in."

Trap shook his head. "You read Doc in. What you know is conjuncture at this point."

47

Aine

I knew something was very wrong when Merrigan and Saylor came into the room.

"Penelope," she began. "Would you mind going next door for a few minutes?"

Pen nodded and rose, meeting my eye as she left.

Merrigan looked from me to Ava and then to Quinn and Saylor. "Striker, Razor, Mercer, and Monk, as well as the rest of the team that left from here yesterday, have all arrived safely in Colombia."

I blinked away the tears that threatened; it looked as though Ava and Quinn were doing the same.

"I have been informed that the missing aircraft was located by DEA agents near the Venezuelan border."

Ava gasped and covered her face with her hands. Merrigan put her hand on her shoulder.

"All we know now is that the plane went down. There were three survivors, who were taken by medevac to a hospital in Magdalena, the closest city in Colombia."

"You said there were three survivors, which means the fourth didn't make it," said Quinn, whose face had gone white.

"As I said, we don't know all the details," Merrigan answered, reaching out for Quinn with her free hand.

"Who was on the plane?" asked Razor's sister.

"Montano 'Onyx' Yáñez, Sofia 'Corazón' Descanso, Landry 'Tackle' Sorenson, and Knox 'Halo' Clarkson."

Merrigan said each name slowly, as if to honor all four of them since we didn't know who had survived and who had not.

I stopped fighting my tears and wept openly. Ava came and sat by my side, crying as hard as I was.

"Striker, Razor, and Monk are being transported to Magdalena now. We'll know more once they've arrived."

Saylor sat on the other side of Ava, and Quinn moved closer to Merrigan.

"Where are my father and Mercer?" she asked.

"They, along with Gunner, will soon be on their way to the hospital as well."

Ava sat up. "Where is Zary?"

"She was napping with the baby," answered 2:15 sounded like Taylor? Saylor. "We thought it best to let her sleep."

"I'll tell her," offered Ava.

Merrigan stood. "If there are no further questions, I need to get back down to the office."

Ava scooted over so we were all as close as we could get on the sofa and held her hand out to Quinn. "Come sit with us," she said.

"Are we hurting you?" Quinn asked me after she sat down.

"I'm okay." The truth was, I couldn't feel much of anything outside of the boulder-sized dread that sat in my stomach.

Someone whom the K19 team had worked with, admired, loved even, had died. In an excruciating way, it drove home how fragile the life they led could be because of the work they did.

"I need to tell my mom," said Saylor, standing. "Do any of you need anything before I go next door?"

I shook my head. "Thank you, though."

"What do we do now?" Ava asked.

"We wait," answered Quinn.

48

Aine
Two Weeks Later

I sat on the sofa with Griffin and watched as the evening news reported on the assassination of Colombia's President Petro Santos, who in recent weeks, had been linked to the Cali drug cartel.

Carlos "Mao" Deodar, leader of that cartel, had also been assassinated on the same day. While he was killed in a different part of Colombia, it was believed the two deaths were related.

The country where Griffin had been only two weeks before, was in utter chaos. Santos' second-in-command was arrested for conspiracy to commit murder when his role in the president's death was discovered.

An emergency election was called, in which former President Francisco Marquez was predicted to be re-elected. If so, it was expected he'd take office immediately and restore normalcy to the embattled nation.

There was no mention, in this broadcast or any other, of the plane that went down in the Colombian National Forest, nor of the death in that crash.

Griffin told me very little, other than that Onyx had been taken to George Washington University Hospital in Washington, DC, as soon as he was stabilized enough to be transported. He remained in a coma still, which was why he and I had returned to his McLean, Virginia, condo and would stay here until his teammate's condition improved.

Both Tackle and Halo, who had sustained surprisingly few injuries, had been released from medical care once they'd returned to the States.

The two had met with Griffin almost every day since we'd arrived in McLean, as had Monk, whom he'd said was also in town, waiting for Onyx to come out of his coma.

Ava and Tabon had gone back to Yachats a few days after the team returned from Colombia; Zary and Gunner were living on his island in the middle of Chesapeake Bay; and Quinn and Mercer had moved into their new house in Paso Robles, which had been miraculously completed in weeks rather than months.

Penelope said that when she returned to New York after Thanksgiving, Tara had moved out of their shared Manhattan apartment and left no forwarding address or contact information.

I worried about Tara every day, to the point that Griffin had stepped in and told me he'd do everything he could to locate her. A few days later, he said that Halo had agreed to find her, and as soon as he heard something, I would be the first to know.

I'd asked about paying him, but Griffin immediately shot me down and refused to discuss how his teammate was being compensated for finding my friend.

As hard as it was to tell him, I'd confessed that I believed Tara may have taken his aunt's bracelet and that I was devastated I'd lost something so precious to him. His response had been that there wasn't anything as precious to him as I was, and he'd get me another bracelet.

"Are you okay?" I asked when Griffin leaned forward and put his head in his hands.

He sat back against the sofa and put his arm around my shoulders.

"Are you sure you wouldn't rather be in Yachats for Christmas?" he asked.

"Is that where you'll be?"

"You know I can't leave until Onyx wakes up. I'm sorry, sweetheart."

"Then, no, I wouldn't rather be in Yachats." It wasn't the first time he'd asked, and I doubted it would be the last. "I want to be wherever you are whenever I can be," I told him now and every other time he'd brought it up.

"What time is your appointment tomorrow?"

"I can go in anytime since it's just a blood draw."

Griffin rested his hand on my belly as though by doing so, everything would turn out okay.

While the doctor in California had told me to wait six weeks before getting certain tests done, the doctor I'd seen here at the hospital for my post-surgery checkup told me she didn't see the need to postpone it.

Two days ago, I'd gone in for my first round of fertility tests. The numbers reported from that round would be considered baseline, and the numbers from tomorrow's blood draw would indicate how well my reproductive system was functioning.

"If the numbers are discouraging this month, we'll continue to test for at least four months to see if there is any change," the doctor said when Griffin and I met in her office after my checkup.

49

Striker

I opened the door when I saw the mail carrier walk up three days after Aine had completed her first full round of fertility testing.

"I have a certified letter for Griffin Ellis," the man said.

"That's me." I already had my ID out and handed it over before signing the green card.

What was inside the envelope I held in my hand would determine my fate along with Aine's and the children we may or may not have one day.

I took the unopened envelope inside and set it on the kitchen counter.

"It came?" Aine asked when she walked up beside me.

I sighed and rolled my shoulders. "It did."

"Are you sure you want to wait?"

"Your appointment with Dr. Fredrickson is in two days. She agreed that if we had my results back prior to that, we'd discuss both then."

"I know. I'm just saying that if you don't want to wait, I'm okay with it."

"Do you want me to open it today?"

Aine shook her head. "They're your results, Griffin."

"Then, we'll wait together."

I dropped Aine off at the hospital entrance and went to park the car. A winter storm had blanketed the DC area in snow, which meant it would be a white Christmas, but it also meant the temperatures were frigid. I checked my pocket to be sure I'd remembered the envelope that contained my DNA results.

Aine and I had talked late into the night about how we'd handle whichever scenario was given to us at today's appointment. While I'd expected Aine to become emotional about it, I was far more so than she was.

I took a deep breath, said a silent prayer, and got out of the car. The prayer wasn't for me; it was for the beautiful, brave woman who waited inside. The one who made me promise that, regardless of the news we received, we'd face life's celebrations and challenges together.

When I walked through the door and saw her waiting, I took another deep breath. How could someone as wondrously perfect as Aine have fallen in love with me? I took her hand in mine and walked over to the elevator.

"It'll be okay, Griffin," she said once the door closed behind us and we rode to the third floor alone.

"That's what you keep telling me." I leaned down and kissed her. "You know I love you."

"I do." She winked.

We were early for our appointment, so we sat and waited ten long minutes before Aine's name was called.

"Dr. Fredrickson will be right with you," said the nurse who led us into an office rather than an exam room.

"Hello," the doctor said, coming in and closing the door behind her. "It's nice to see you both," she added before shaking each of our hands.

She sat down and opened a folder that sat on the desk. "Did you receive your results?" she asked, looking at me.

"I did," I answered, handing her the unopened envelope.

Epilogue

Aine

"*Tabon, they're here*!" shouted Ava, coming to the front door and throwing her arms around me.

"Good to see you," I heard him say to Griffin while Ava and I continued to hug each other.

"I can't go this long without seeing you ever again. Do you understand me?" Ava said with tears in her eyes. "I can't believe it's only been five months. It seems more like five years."

It had been difficult to be away from my twin for Christmas, especially for the first time, but we'd managed by having video calls almost daily.

"Where's Sam?"

"Right here," said our mother, bringing her grandson over to me.

My eyes filled with tears. "He's gotten so big." I'd been worried Sam wouldn't remember me, but he came right to me and put his little arms around my neck, slobbering on my cheek. "I think he remembers me."

"Of course he does," said Ava.

“Come inside,” said Tabon . “Ava’s got quite a spread prepared.”

“That looks like enough to feed thirty people!” I gasped when I saw all the serving dishes full of food.

“I hope so,” Ava answered, pointing to the sign that hung behind us.

Oh, Babies!
Coming soon!
The McNamara-Ellis Twins!

I looked at Griffin, who was beaming back at me.

“Am I ever happy that it’s you two having twins,” said Tabon, shaking Griffin’s hand.

“Twins run in our family, sweetheart. There’s nothing to say we won’t have our own set someday,” Ava said to her husband.

Tabon put his hand on his wife’s belly. “This is just one though, right?”

“You’ve been at all the ultrasounds with me. If there were two in here, you’d know.” Ava looked out the window. “Quinn and Mercer are here!” she shouted.

“They are?” I asked, turning around to see them driving in.

"Everyone is coming," said Ava, holding both of my hands. "We're all so happy for you and Griffin."

Ava looked at my hand. "Hey—where's the ring?"

"My fingers are too fat, so I wear it here." I showed her the diamond and garnet ring I wore on a chain around my neck.

"It's gorgeous!" gasped Ava. "You did good," she said, turning toward Griffin.

—Striker—

"Can I get you a beer?" asked Razor.

"Please." I followed him into the kitchen.

"Congratulations again," he said, clinking his bottle against the one he'd handed me. "When's the big day?"

"We haven't decided yet. Aine says she wants to wait until after the twins are born. I'd marry her today if she'd agree to it."

"That's how it was for Ava and me, although it was her idea not to wait. I wanted to make sure she didn't regret having a big wedding, and all she cared about was that all of our friends were here to celebrate with us."

"I met Aine that day."

"I remember."

"If I hadn't let Monk drag me to your wedding, I might not be standing here today."

"How is Monk?"

"Determined to help Onyx recover, to the exclusion of everything else in his life."

"Saylor and the girls will be here today. I'll warn you that she might ask about him."

"Thanks for the heads-up, although I don't know what I'll tell her."

"I hear ya. I've run out of things to say myself."

"There you are," said Aine, walking up to me and putting her arm around my waist. "Ava just told me that everyone is going to be in town for the long Easter weekend."

"Yeah? Everybody?"

"Almost everybody," she said. The situation with both Onyx and Monk, along with Tara, was something we talked about often.

I leaned forward so my mouth was next to her ear. "I'm sorry. I didn't mean to make you sad."

Aine sighed. "You didn't. Anyway, we were thinking..."

Razor laughed and clapped me on the back. "What did I tell you?"

"What was that about?" Aine asked when Razor walked out.

"He was talking about marrying your sister and how he wanted to wait in case she needed time to plan it, but she didn't. I told him I'd marry you tomorrow if you'd agree to it."

She smiled. "I do."

"You do?"

"I absolutely do."

Keep reading for a sneak peek
at the next book in the
K19 Security Solutions Series—
MONK!

Prologue

Monk

The ICU nurses were used to me showing up each morning without saying a word to anyone and then leaving the same way. So, like every other day of the last twenty-three, I walked past the desk silently when I left to get some dinner. Sure, it was Christmas, but I really didn't give a shit about holidays, especially this year, with my friend in intensive care.

When I got off the elevator on the main floor, I buttoned up the peacoat that had belonged to my grandfather, put on my beanie, and pulled it down over my ears. I reached into my pockets, took out my gloves, and put the left one on first. I was about to put on the right when I felt my cell phone vibrate. I pulled it out and swiped the screen.

Look up, it said; I did.

"Hi," said the woman who'd sent it, slowly approaching me.

"Saylor." Given I was unable to decide whether to tell her how good it was to see her or ask her what in the hell she was doing there, I said nothing more than her name.

"Merry Christmas, Monk."

"What are you doing here?"

"My mom, the girls, and I are spending Christmas in Annapolis again this year."

Last year, I'd been with Saylor and her family at the same place. One of the founding partners of K19 Security Solutions, a private security and intelligence firm where I was a junior partner, had hosted a Christmas celebration. Not only had I been there, but Onyx had too.

"How's Onyx?" Saylor asked as though she knew what I was thinking.

"No change."

"I'm sorry, Monk. I was praying for a Christmas miracle."

I eased the glove off my left hand, put them both in my pocket, and then stepped forward. I gripped Saylor's nape with one hand, wrapped my other arm around her waist, and kissed her. It wasn't a chaste kiss. I didn't waste time with shit like that. Not with her. I tightened my hold so Saylor's body was flush with mine and deepened our kiss.

I pulled back and looked in her eyes. "I'm sorry—"

She put her fingertips on my lips. "Don't."

No one was ever as easy on me as Saylor. And no one deserved to be hard on me more than she did.

"Where were you going?"

"Dinner."

She tucked her arm in mine. "Good. I'm hungry."

My loft was a ten-minute walk from the hospital. If I were alone, I'd stop and eat somewhere on the way.

"It's cold."

"I'm okay to walk," she said, snuggling up against me when we went outside.

In the almost year and a half since I met Saylor, we'd been apart far more than together, and yet she was able to read me like no one else ever had. Two words, and she knew what I was asking. It always surprised me, but it shouldn't.

"This is nice," she said when I opened the door to my loft and invited her in.

"Thanks." I'd gotten the three-bedroom unit because I wanted to be on the top floor of the building and I wanted a view. I didn't care about it being too big for me or about the price.

When the listing agent offered to throw in the staging furniture for a nominal fee, I took her up on it. Everything else in it, I'd ordered online. I didn't have time to shop, not that I would've anyway. I spent every day at George Washington University Hospital, waiting for my friend to come out of the coma he'd been in since surviving a plane crash almost a month ago.

I took Saylor's coat and hung it in the closet with mine and then walked into the kitchen and opened the fridge. I kept it well stocked, again by ordering online and having the groceries delivered.

Saylor came up behind me and wrapped her arms around my waist. "When did you last eat?" she asked.

"Lunch. You said you were hungry."

"I can wait."

I closed the refrigerator door and led her into the master bedroom.

About the Author

I gave myself the gift of writing a book for my birthday one year. A few short years and thirty-plus books later, I've hit a couple of best-seller lists and have had the time of my life. The joy for me is in writing them, but nothing makes me happier than hearing from a reader who tells me I've made her laugh or cry or gasp or hold her breath or stay up all night because she can't put my book down.

The women I write are self-confident, strong, with wills of their own, and hearts as big as the Colorado sky. The men are sublimely sexy, seductive alphas who rise to the challenge of capturing the sweet soul of a woman whose heart they'll hold in the palm of their hand forever. Add in a couple of neck-snapping twists and turns, a page-turning mystery, and a swoon-worthy HEA, and you'll be holding one of my books in your hands.

I love to hear from my readers. You can contact me at heather@heatherslade.com

To keep up with my latest news and releases, please visit my website at www.heatherslade.com to sign up for my newsletter.

MORE FROM AUTHOR HEATHER SLADE

Butler Ranch

Prequel: *Kade's Worth*

Book One: *Brodie*

Book Two: *Maddox*

Book Three: *Naughton*

Book Four: *Mercer*

Book Five: *Kade*

K19 Security Solutions

Book One: *Razor*

Book Two: *Gunner*

Book Three: *Mistletoe*

Book Four: *Mantis*

Book Five: *Dutch*

Book Six: *Striker*

Book Seven: *Monk*

Book Eight: *Halo*

Book Nine: *Tackle*

Coming soon:

Book Ten: *Onyx*

Military Intelligence Section 6

Book One: *Shiver*

Book Two: *Wilder*

Book Three: *Pinch*

Book Four: *Shadow*

The Invincibles

Book One: *Decked*

Book Two: *Edged*

Book Three: *Grinded*

Book Four: *Riled*

Book Five: *Smoked*

Book Six: *Bucked*

Coming soon:

Book Seven: *Irished*

Roaring Fork Ranch

Coming soon:

Book One: *Roughstock*

Book Two: *Rockstar*

Cowboys of Crested Butte

Book One: *Fall for Me*

Book Two: *Dance with Me*

Book Three: *Kiss Me Cowboy*

Book Four: *Stay with Me*

Book Five: *Win Me Over*

Cocky Hero Club

Undercover Agent

KB Worlds

Everyday Heroes: *Handled*